# Hades' Redemption

Dixie Jo Jarchow

Published by Wintergreen Books, 2023.

HADES' REDEMPTION

**First edition. March 16, 2023.**



ISBN: 979-8215807644

Written by Dixie Jo Jarchow.

To Maggie with many thanks!

# Chapter One

As the first chill fingers of fall touched the glacier moraine town of Fell, Wisconsin, the mist of a million pine trees spewed their gametes into the air, muting the bright sunlight and gilding everything a hazy gold. A Sunday designed for ennui with pre-season football just beginning, and the preacher passed through those eternal goal posts to his eternal reward from a stroke and planted in the cemetery.

Into that beautiful stillness, two more bodies arrived in the tiny hamlet within an hour of each other: one body was dead, and the other was alive. People drifted into the coffee shop to chew over the sparse details like hard gristle on a steak.

"First body I recall in the quarry, though that hole's been there as long as I can remember," old man Johnson pronounced. Everyone nodded, sipping their steaming black coffee in a lame attempt to justify holding onto a table throughout the morning. The town's economy revolved around the quarry and news concerning it fascinated them like gossip about a cousin.

The corpse rose from the deep frigid water of the quarry as if conjured for the delight of the two local boys who found it. The Kratz kids, Tommy and Joe, rode their bicycles into town yelling about a naked girl floating in the quarry. Everyone trooped out to their trucks and drove behind the Sheriff's squad car. The foreman, Dan Plano, a large, solid, serious man produced a gold key from a wad on a heavy ring and opened up the white painted steel fence. He walked the gate back wide to let the vehicles stream past.

There was no question of who did or did not belong at the crime scene. There would have been a lynching if the Sheriff tried to keep any of the town's people out. The quarry was their livelihood and their life's blood. Anything that had to do with it involved them intimately. The Sheriff didn't even try to limit the access.

The quarry looked like a dusty wad of debris thrown onto the verdant woodland that surrounded it. It produced metric tons of gravel as well as a prized fine-grained pink limestone. On this, the Lord's Day, no one was working, and the quarry could have been an alien world, silent and covered in a pervasive pink spray of dust. As people got out of their trucks, their shoes stirred up the particles and a salmon colored cloud rose around them.

They crowded the crumbling edge of the zigzag road that threaded its way to the lower reaches of the quarry. When, in the circle of milky aqua that covered the bottom, they located a splash of pale flesh bobbing across the darkness, they gasped. The young body was thin almost emaciated. Viewed in other circumstances, she could have been a model posed then painted with shades of black, green and blue. Her hair fanned out in a dark corona around her face. The townspeople recoiled from the ferocious beating the woman had suffered. A communal shiver ran through them. No one's child should have to die this hard.

One of the Kratz kids took out a cell phone to take a picture and his mother put her hand over the camera and shook her head. Wasn't right, disrespecting the dead. She belonged to some family, not of Fell, but somewhere. No one would appreciate an image of their kin indecent and vulnerable going out of the internet.

The Sheriff selected three sturdy men to go with him down the winding switchbacks. They grabbed a tarp from a talus pile at the bottom and rolled the body into the worn canvas. The Sheriff sucked deeply on his inhaler and watched the procession. Everyone knew he had bad asthma. It was why they'd made him Sheriff. He couldn't work in the dusty environment of the quarry.

They carried the corpse to the top and waited for the Sheriff to struggle up, although she was light enough for one to do the job. The Sheriff was forty, but had the seamed face of an older man. He wheezed for a minute and then bent over and pulled one edge of the tarp back to expose the girl's head.

"Anyone know her?" He asked.

The crowd took a serious moment to consider, to be sure they didn't recognize her and then shook their collective heads. Her face was a technicolor canvas and part of a cheek had collapsed under the force of the blows. People drew closer, struggling with their ignorance. They wanted to name her but no one called forth recognition.

And that was the most startling revelation. In the cloistered community where everyone knew everything about everyone, she was a stranger. In the minutes since her discovery, she grew from an anonymous corpse to a poor unknown girl, a part of Fell's fabric.

The Sheriff took pictures and emailed them to the authorities in the surrounding towns. The remnants of glacial till that created the rolling hills and valleys isolated neighboring villages from each other. Maybe she came from over the hills. You had to hate someone right down to your soul to beat them like that, they whispered. Who despised this young girl so?

The hearse from Nehring's Funeral Home pulled up, generating a heavy dust cloud that coated the crowd. The Sheriff gave terse instructions to the solemn high school boy who was the star wide receiver for Fell High and drove the wagon weekends for his uncle.

There hadn't been a murder in Fell since 1947 when Selma Milander didn't wait for Bobby Rigan to come home from the Big One and instead married his friend Anthony Rezmissen, a singer who worked the nightclub circuit. Bobby came back from the war without his legs and rolled his wheelchair over to his dad's house to pick up his shotgun. He blew a hole clean through Anthony and then killed himself. Selma had to move away from the accusing stares of her friends and neighbors. That one was open and shut compared to this mystery.

If this young woman wasn't killed in Fell, did that make it their murder or not? If the killing occurred somewhere else and was dumped in the quarry, then it wasn't even their homicide, was it?

Heated discussions ensued as the procession followed the body back to town. CB's were crackling with the longest monologues people had heard in years.

As they got out of their trucks at the coffee shop, a white Cadillac turned at the light, heading towards the church. Every eye tracked its progress.

The crowd knew within that vehicle sat the replacement for the dead priest. Darkened windows prevented serious gawking, but people mumbled a thanks be to God that he'd arrived too late to consider holding a service today.

The past two Sundays without enforced repentance had been a gift from on high.

"Wish they'd held off sending someone until February," was a popular refrain. Worship at 11 interfered with tailgating and the eleven o'clock pre game. The previous priest refused to budge on the time and everyone thought he didn't want an earlier start because he was hung over. They went to church, but they weren't happy, and sneaking out during the last hymn was an exodus akin to Moses and the Jews fleeing Egypt.

That he was a Friar and not an actual priest had people wondering whether he would be staying. When Miss Carolyn left to pick him up at the airport, half the town wagered she would leave him there. People shook their heads and smiled.

Miss Carolyn was of the Bennington family, as much a part of the landscape as the quarry and the coffee shop. Her grandfather was moving west when he discovered an outcrop of cool pink limestone under the rocky soils and began the first dig to supply building stone from Chicago to Washington D.C. Miss Carolyn still controlled a large chunk of the company and therefore the livelihoods of most of the town.

Miss Carolyn liked her religion and her rich brother in New York had used his pull to get her the first priest. Money changed hands, people nodded to each other. It was the way things got done in the city. The priest had represented serious bragging rights over nearby towns, but then the fool crawled into a bottle, causing the stroke that killed him.

She wouldn't be pleased that a naked young woman lay on a stainless steel table in the funeral home this very minute. It might dull her presentation of the Friar. What the hell was a Friar anyway? People weren't sure if they should be proud or ashamed to have one.

"Priests are hard to come by. We shall see about this Friar," Miss Carolyn told the congregation. No one doubted that if he didn't suit, he would be returned, postage paid.

Back in the coffee shop, the talk had turned to whether the murder belonged to Fell or not. It was enough of a slight they couldn't get a replacement priest for the one that up and drank himself to a stroke, God rest his soul, now their own homicide might be relegated to the not so glamorous status of a dump site. It was not to be tolerated. She was viewed as proprietary and became "Our girl."

They swarmed into the coffee shop like bees to a hive and listened a spell for updates before drifting off to do their Sunday chores. Debate about the new Friar was put on the back burner until more information was available. There was plenty of excitement in Fell without him.

# Chapter Two

"Are you humming along with the song or growling?" Miss Carolyn snapped. Her tight cap of curly white hair jutted over a sun darkened face with the texture of a brown paper bag. Her soft, worn blue flannel shirt and ancient jeans conveyed a relaxed comfort with herself. That she came from money wouldn't have crossed his mind by looking at the thin woman.

"I'm fine," Friar Hades' teeth clenched against the onslaught of country twanging on the radio. His tastes ran more to strident rock guitar. This had to count as a form of penance for him. Like a car wreck he couldn't look away from, he listened to the story of the girl who stole the singer's dog, pickup truck and heart.

"You're sweating like a hog and I've known goats who smelled better. Aren't you allowed to wash your robe?" Miss Carolyn complained.

"I washed them just this week at Father Xavier's command. I wasn't aware Wisconsin was this lush." He kept his voice low and pleasant.

"Another month and everything will be buried in a foot of snow. I have to be honest, I'm angry as a hornet that I only rate a Friar instead of a priest. You don't like little boys, do you?" She spared a look at his face as she drove. At least the regular side was facing her, not the disfigured side.

"I like them but I don't LIKE them."

"Little girls?"

"Same and same."

"My brother dumps a shitload of money on the church," she began.

"I know," Hades reviewed the instructions Father Xavier gave him before he'd left for Fell.

"You don't realize how important this posting is, Hades." Father Xavier's thick, soft robes swirled as he paced back and forth in Hades' tiny cell.

"I do because you keep telling me." Hades kept his head bowed, trying not to be resentful of his own rough wool clothing. He could have had the softer combed wool but chose the harder road at every turn as part of his journey towards salvation.

"Smiths Bennington is a self-made millionaire and his sister wanted a priest. You will be small consolation. Do your best. Be pleasant Get along with people. Smile once in a while." Hades grinned at the priest.

"Dear God, no, don't smile. Try for pensive and attentive. Think pleasant thoughts. And try not to have those screaming nightmares." The priest shuddered while he imparted instructions. Hades had moved the furniture out of his eight-foot by eight foot cell and blocked the heat vent. The concrete floor bit into his bony knees when he prayed and it was horrible to sleep on with the one thin blanket he allowed himself. He tried not to dwell on the worse places he'd slept in the war.

"Are you listening or just daydreaming, son? So what's the deal with your face?" Miss Carolyn kept her eyes on the road. His attention snapped back to her.

At least she was blunt and came out and asked him about his face. "I was a recon scout in the army before I became a Friar. I was captured and tortured by insurgents. Battery acid," he said in a monotone. It wasn't anything he could talk about easily, even now it gave him a start when he saw himself in a mirror.

"Couldn't they fix it?"

"No." Between tissue damage and the thick melted skin, the surgeons shook their heads. He was ok with it. God didn't care that he looked like a side show freak.

"Do you play sports? We could use a coach at the high school."

"Coaching what?"

"You name it, we need it. Ah, there's the house. It's nothing that great but it's free and will keep the ticks off your bedroll." She turned in and drove past a postcard beautiful white clapboard church and stopped at a tiny cabin snugged up to the base of the mountain.

"Ticks?" He really hoped she was joking. He hadn't been bothered by bugs until Iraq when the rumors of the sand spiders turned out to be true. Spiders the size of dinner plates would chase you to stay in your shadow where it was cooler. He'd seen the bodies where their razor mandibles had chewed an oval into the side of their host and fed. Soldiers killed them on sight and all living things feared them.

Since then, he'd mistrusted and avoided bugs, despite spending a small eternity in the jungle while ravenous swarms of bugs fed on him, one drop of blood at a time. Did he prefer the jungle wars or the desert wars? Sand everywhere and that terrible thirst. The torturers were of a higher quality in the desert regions, he felt, although he might have been prejudiced. Both had their good and bad points.

He rubbed his arms. In the last breath of summer, the dark pines stretched up to the heavens, dark, tick laden pines. He sighed. They would, no doubt, join forces with the sand spiders in his nightmares and chase him relentlessly through the sleepless nights. Perhaps out here on the edge of town, no one would be bothered by his screams.

Miss Carolyn stood in front of the truck watching him through the windshield, a frown on her face. He jumped out of the vehicle and mounted the steps to stand near her on the porch. It wasn't too nice, simple, plain. Just the right thing for someone adding penance in small doses to even out all the death on his side of the scale. It wasn't enough but every bit helped. The sooner he could start saving souls and make some serious entries on the positive side of God's ledger, the better.

The small porch in the front of the cabin sloped at an angle with crooked steps that needed work. He would start a list of repairs to make. The porch sagged, wood groaning when he stepped upon it.

"Father wasn't much at upkeep." Carolyn apologized.

The front of the cabin had a nice, but small front window looking toward the church. The forest started at the back screened-in porch and climbed into the sky. It was like a seat in God's own cathedral. It looked restful.

He opened the door and dust motes danced a welcome to him. The cabin opened into a small sitting room with a couch and a chair that held deep butt imprints.

"Father Kennedy a large man?"

"Nice guess." Miss Carolyn walked through and Hades followed her. She ran her fingers along the counter of the small galley kitchen and smiled. "We had a woman and her daughter come in and clean earlier this week. Get it ready for you."

"I appreciate that."

"We can keep them on if you'd like. Come every two weeks or so to do the heavy stuff."

"No, that won't be necessary." He would keep his own house. He didn't have any possession to mess it up. Sloth was one of the seven deadly ones.

"I'm sorry we don't have anything bigger for you."

"I like it. It's the largest place I've even lived," he gestured around the room.

"This little place? Where all have you lived?"

"Oh, here and there." He didn't want to recount his life's story for this woman. It depressed him enough, no reason to bring her to the edges of his own personal hell.

She glared at him, lips pursed together in a line until he looked away.

"So, sitting room, kitchen, bathroom and bedroom, laundry in this little room off the screened-in porch. Doesn't look like you're a clothes horse. I made sure the kitchen is stocked. I look forward to hearing you preach this Sunday."

"Preaching? I'm not sure if I'm qualified to preach."

"Well, just talk then. Maybe about your travels," she suggested.

He ground his teeth together. Which part should he start with? When the Iraqi insurgents captured him and the fuckers dripped acid on his face? How lucky he felt to still have both eyes? Or the satisfaction of putting a bullet in the Death Triangle on an enemies' face, that sweet spot above the eyebrows direct center. Or pulling leeches off in the jungles and eating them while he waited interminable hours for a signal from base to move forward into danger?

"I'm not really your sweetness and light kind of guy. My goal is to bring people to God by example."

"Well, we didn't bring you all the way out here just because we could. The people of this little community need someone to speak to them, to help them find their way, and you got the job." Anger made her eyes look darker and set the lines on her face. He looked down at the fine white hair on her head, sparse at the crown but she did a good job of hiding it.

"I'm not a preacher, I'm a Friar. Friars don't preach and preachers don't ah, do what we do."

"Well what exactly do you do?" She faced him, hands on her bird bone hips.

"I lead by example. Friars do good works across a wide geographical region. We fast. We do penance." He was gesturing and walking back and forth.

"Well, this Sunday, your penance is to preach. You've got a few days so I'd say you better start working on your sermon now." She slammed the door on her way out and he wondered that the hinges held. He held his breath while the dust from the door settled.

A sermon? He'd never given a sermon in his life. The droning monotones he'd listened to as he went through the Orders to become a Friar were designed to test your sanity. He didn't even remember any of them. Maybe he should talk about his face. It was the most visible scar of his life in the military but by no means the only one.

How long did a sermon have to be anyway? Ten minutes? Five? As long as they had plenty of hymns, he didn't see why he couldn't do it. The penance angle appealed to him. Doing something that he truly didn't want to do. Well, if it was what God wanted, who was he to say no?

Think of all the souls he might reach.

He pulled a small table to sit in front of the window. Hell, he picked up the desk and put it on the porch. It was too nice to be inside. The weather hovered around the 60s, but he had always liked it cold. He could tolerate that better than the heat. Gummed up your rifle when it got too hot and the frigid air gave a truer bullet trajectory.

He needed paper. He went back into the house and went through the drawers in the kitchen. About halfway through his search, he found some blank paper and a pencil.

Sitting on the porch in front of the little desk, staring at the deep green forest, he wrote, "Hello, I'm Friar Hades..." He stared at the paper then off into the trees for several minutes.

Damn this was hard work! What he really needed was a beer. He went back into the house to look in the refrigerator. God be praised, they had beer. Shock Top, he'd never heard of the brand but was grateful nonetheless.

After a beer, his mind was still an empty canvas. Running might help clear his mind. He pulled a pair of running shorts and his shoes out of the duffle bag and laced up his shoes. Shrugging out of his robe to pull on a beat up T-shirt that said, "Running with the Buffaloes" and stretching a little as he walked towards the door. He wasn't a fan of too much stretching when his muscles were cold. Relieved there wasn't a mirror in the bedroom, he thanked God for small favors. As difficult as it was for others to see his face, it reminded Hades of the interminable days and nights at the mercy of his torturers.

Time to look at this little town. Maybe his sermon would write itself in his head while he ran. Sometimes, problems worked like that.

At first, the priests at the New York rectory had forbidden him to run. That was something he hadn't expected when he chose to become a Friar. Running long and strong kept the visions at bay. Not important religious visions, visions of the raw sewage of his life before his calling. He tried exercising to exhaustion in other ways in his cell, but nothing replaced running for keeping the nightmares at bay.

The nightmares became unbearable and then became waking nightmares or daymares as the psychologist called them. He began to have trouble distinguishing real from imaginary.

An unwary UPS man stumbled into one of his waking fantasies and Hades strung him up in the kitchen. Only the screaming of the cook had saved the man. Hades received a special dispensation to run so he could force the monsters to retreat back to his dreams.

Even on the weeks he logged over one hundred miles, he still had night terrors and would wake screaming, fighting battles that were long lost.

He started at a medium pace to warm up, but stopped when he got to the end of the road that the church was on. Which way was the town? He couldn't remember much of the drive here, just that stupid song rolling through his brain. His memory often selected what it would retain and what it wouldn't: another problem from his time in the military. When he thought about how detailed and vivid his memories of the savagery were, maybe his brain refused to save anything else.

He chose to go right and pounded down the two lane highway. An ancient white delivery truck appeared around the curve coming towards him but in the other lane. Hades smiled at the large "O" that the elderly man's mouth made as he saw Hades' face. Old tires protested the swerve, as the man braked later than he should have. Hades was already apexing the next corner, maximizing the downhill. He wasn't getting any younger. Maybe he should stop and stretch after another minute.

The scenery was gorgeous and so different from New York City. Fall was tipping the trees with color and the temperature around 60 degrees Fahrenheit was perfect for running. The haze in the air gave everything an unreal glow, but made him hack when the mist of pine went into his lungs. The road sloped upwards at a steep angle after the curve and Hades smiled. Hills, my God how he loved them. Nothing like hills to give your body a workout and drive sin from a body. Sweat sluiced off his body and it cooled him quickly.

A bridge held the top of the rise and he evaluated it as a strategic target. The heavy, corroded metal signaled frequent use and Hades imagined that as a recon scout he would destroy this bridge as soon as possible to cut supply routes. A part of his mind calculated the amount and placement of the explosives. He shook his head to clear it. As he got to the top, he could see two young girls sitting close to each other on one side of the bridge; early teens judging by their stick thin legs. Long brown hair blew back like streamers at a town fair.

One of the girls caught his movement and rotated towards him. First, shock then that expression was replaced by fear. He ran past them before they could comment or greet him. He waved a hand in acknowledgement that said he couldn't stop. Much like bikers used to signal each other, runners on a workout would just gesture. It wasn't rude if you knew that but he worried. First impressions were important.

They had drummed that into him in Friar school. He figured he didn't have a chance at a good first impression with his half-ruined face.

As the road curved and sloped away from the bridge he came upon the town, snug and picturesque in a depression between two ridges, circled protectively by pine trees. Hades marveled at the pines, straight and tall with no branches lower than 30 feet off the ground. He could make out "Fell, Wisconsin" on a battered wooden sign as he raced past but he couldn't make out the other stuff on the sign, champions of something so long ago it had faded.

He was through the town in less than a minute. A small cluster of stores clung to the main street, no doubt named, "Main Street." He ran on, and the road swept into an upward climb that caused his calves to threaten cramping.

What did people do here to make a living? He would have to find out and also look at the surrounding communities. He was responsible for the souls of each of these pockets of humanity. Hades stopped running at the top of the ridge and knelt in prayer before he stretched.

God would make him up to the task of ministering to the small communities.

He ran back at a blistering pace. He didn't see anyone which struck him as odd. In New York City, you couldn't get away from the crush of people. Even when he ran at two in the morning to fight off a bad night terror, people were working and walking around the city like insomniacs.

When he got back to the cabin, he spent a long time stretching until he realized he was avoiding the sermon. He took a quick shower, mindful of Father Xavier's warning to shower often. His bald head felt strange. Should he keep it or let his hair grow? He liked the idea of bald but the upkeep bothered him as a vanity. Hair, it would be at least until people started calling him, "Jesus" again.

He put on his robe again, feeling the rough wool against his naked skin. He knew Friars frequently opted for softer material, still wool but not as scratchy, but he couldn't make himself do it. Some simply put a t-shirt and underwear on under it. Hades liked wearing just the robe. It was just him and God was how he saw it.

He sat at the tiny desk on the porch. The afternoon was clear and crystalline. The sermon came to him and he wrote it down the way God sent it.

The subtle noises of the hills lulled him as he sat. He reached up a hand to rub his neck; it was hard as a rock. He rolled his head once, grimacing at the cracking noises that reverberated in his head.

Crickets sang and birds argued as the temperature dropped into the delightful fifties. Miss Carolyn wasn't as frightening as he'd expected. She wasn't what he expected at all, to be fair. He expected a chorus of somber faced men in suits would be waiting to meet the plane, not a diminutive white haired lady with vinegar in her veins. Miss Carolyn's no-nonsense in your face persona worked well for him. He didn't have the energy to waste dissembling or figuring out the undercurrents of people's meaning. God's work awaited. Nothing else mattered.

His shoulders relaxed and the tension left his upper back. Somewhere, water bubbled and ran down the dark rock face behind him. A sense of calmness seeped into his skin and Hades took a deep breath of the cool air as the sun swept below the hill in front of him. Although he judged it to be early evening, at most, he went inside and hung up his robe, brushed his teeth and prayed for an hour on the cool, unforgiving wooden plank floor before he went to bed. At the rectory, he started out sleeping bare-assed naked. A smoldering fire in the common room fireplace caused the alarms to blare and Hades had catapulted out of bed and run into the common room.

He shook his head and smiled. You wouldn't think grown men would be so squeamish about the human body, made by God. Since then, he slept in a t-shirt and boxers.

Tonight, sleep eluded him. He rolled off of the bed and did one hundred push-ups and one hundred sit-ups. He sat in half lotus and did his breathing meditation. After an hour, he brought down the pillow and blanket and made his bed on the rough plank floor. He was asleep in moments.

He woke as dawn colored the top of the ridge in front of his house with rose tones. Hades lay motionless on the floor a moment, unsure what woke him. His Army training taught him to wake instantly, fully alert but not betray himself. He opened his eyes after exploring the room with his senses for intruders. He got up and padded to the kitchen.

The clock in the kitchen above the sink showed five o'clock. He downed a glass of water so cold his throat burned and checked out the front door, but no early parishioners were seeking his discourse. A run, perhaps? He stepped into his running shorts and a thin singlet, an ultra light shirt that wicked the sweat away from his body. He pulled a battered pair of running shoes out of his duffle and tied them on.

On Sunday, he stood, legs shaking under his robe, in front of the congregation.

"I'm a Friar. Friars belong to a province or area, not a church. I'm not used to giving sermons. I've been told you all want some words of comfort but I'm not here for that. I am here to remind you of where you're failing. Don't get comfortable. A life with God isn't about comfort. It's about doing your best to be a good person.

"If I see you sinning, don't think I won't call you on it. Same goes for me. I'm no better than you, worse than probably than all of you if you knew me better. You see me sinning; you come up to my face and put my feet back on the right path. I may hate you for a minute but I'll thank you for an eternity.

"I know you're wondering what happened to my face. I was a soldier of man before I became a soldier of God. This is what men do to other men. It pains me every day and I thank God for it. It's a constant reminder of what I was, what I did and what I can be instead.

"I know my words are rough. I'm on the rough side of humanity. I've seen the ugly underside of what people do to each other. I've done horrible things, but I'm here to tell you that's over.

"I belong to God, body and soul, and so do you whether you realize it or not. I'm here because God wants me here. I'm here to remind you that God wants you here too."

He sat. It was strange to be up in front of everyone. Sweat dripped from his armpits under his robe and wound its way to his belly. He worked on his sermon all week and ran. After the sermon, there would be time enough to meet everyone and get the skinny on Fell. He knew he had been in avoidance mode but he rationalized it as a strategy to get more people to church, if only to satisfy their curiosity.

During the week, Miss Carolyn kept him busy with the daily duties of a priest in the church. She went over the books with him and supplies that needed to be ordered. He had a newfound respect for priests and secretaries after a few days. His head was spinning with details of white glue, construction paper and who knew the holy host wafers cost so much?

Hades thought it was more to keep him from running away than anything else. Miss Carolyn hadn't wanted him here in Fell but now she seemed determined to keep him. Well, he'd done it, given his first sermon. No one had laughed or run out of the church. That was a good sign, wasn't it?

The woman at the organ began the next hymn and he could see people fumbling for their hymnals. Some just sat staring at him. He stared back. God had nothing to hide.

He picked up his hymnal and found the page. He forgot to turn his microphone off and his singing boomed out over the congregation. A toddler burst into tears and someone laughed before another shushed him. Hades fumbled for the small switch and resumed singing when he knew it was off. He was a tone-deaf, but enthusiastic singer. He loved to sing, felt it brought him closer to the spirit. While in New York, he was shocked when he realized people moved away from him during the singing portion of the service, but he was singing to God so they could stuff it. Here might be a different story.

He gave the benediction after the final hymn. "Dear God, bring these people closer to your fold. Help root out evil and put their feet upon your path. Help them watch over me and keep me from singing. Amen." He paused a moment when a thundering "AMEN" came from the congregation. "Sinning, I meant," he amended.

He shook hands and tried to count how many people peeled off and went down the outside aisles to avoid him. He lost count.

There was a coffee and cookie reception in the basement. Oreos! He took one and then set it before him. Should he deny himself?

"Come on, Friar Hades, it's an Oreo. I can't see that leading you into sin." Carolyn Bennington sat next to him.

"It starts with an Oreo and then pretty soon gluttony." He put the delicious confection under his paper napkin.

"I heard you've been running some serious miles. You can probably stand a few Oreos. They aren't real Oreos anyway, generic. You looked like you were going to pass out up there. You did well though. I like a little fire with my brimstone. I liked that bit of humor at the end of your sermon. Someone who doesn't take themselves too seriously could be a nice change of pace."

Hades popped the sweet cookie into his mouth to keep from confessing it wasn't intended humor. He savored the explosion of sugar.

After Miss Carolyn sat down next to him, people drifted over and introduced themselves. Hades was soon lost in a blur of names and faces. During a short break while the next group of parishioners worked up the courage to meet him, he stood up and she gave him a typed list of reminders.

"Leave a list of groceries you want on the desk in the office. Someone will pick up supplies once every two weeks. I can give you Father Kennedy's schedule, if you like. On Sundays, we watch football so that's why the service is at 9:30 so everyone can get home to watch the Pack by 11. It used to be later but since you weren't here yet, the board changed it. A big point in your favor, I must say. I'd accuse you of using strategy to win the congregation over, but I don't think you're that devious."

He took a quick breath to protest that he hadn't changed the time of worship. He'd been told when it was but then he realized she was giving him every advantage she could.

She paused and looked at him. "Maybe I've underestimated you on that. We'll see. Tuesday, he did the hospital and home bound visits. Wednesday and Thursday he worked on sermons. Friday and Saturday were his days off."

"Doesn't seem like much to keep a person busy," Hades said dubiously.

"Fell doesn't need much. Just a sermon on Sundays and a visit if someone is ill. A few words at funerals. A marriage here and there."

Hades turned the single page over to find it blank. Fell needed him more than it knew. He slipped it into a pocket inside his woolen robe.

Hades felt observed; not the casual curious stare but a calculated evaluation. Hades stood up and swiveled to face a slim man in a tailored suit leaning against a wall. He stood out like a piece of sharp glass among gravel. He used the camouflage of the crush of people picking up cookies to shield his scrutiny. The man slouched against the wall concealing his true height. Hades judged his to be just a bit taller than he was, probably six feet three. Hades balanced on the balls of his feet in preparation for a fight. He breathed out, emptying his lungs of air and relaxed. Where was the danger here in the church basement? Damn. He could talk himself out of it, but the animal part of him that had survived a hundred such encounters wasn't fooled. Somewhere deep inside him, the predator growled.

The man smiled and pushed himself off the wall.

"Inspiring sermon, Friar Hades, is it?" Perfect teeth and sparkling eye coupled with a firm handshake; salesman popped into his mind. Salesman for the Devil.

"Yes, thank you, and you are?"

"Carson Smith. Welcome to our little slice of heaven on Earth, Friar. Those were some wonderful words. People around here aren't used to getting their hand slapped. I wonder how long they'll put up with it." He pulled up a metal folding chair and they both sat down.

Almost before his butt touched the seat, a teenaged girl appeared with fresh coffee for the man.

"Why thank you, Brittany." He graced the girl with a smile and patted her hand. She giggled and dimpled for him like he was royalty and maybe around here, he was. His clothes were cut better than anyone else's.

"Are you here for a while?" Asked Carson. Another girl thundered up with a plate of cookies and he smiled at her, too. She hurried over to the first girl and Hades noted how they stood rapt watching Smith, talking in animated tones. Puppy love.

"Until I turn to ashes and dust, as far as I know."

Carson took an Oreo from the plate and twisted it. Ever so slowly, he licked the soft cream out of the middle and met Hades' eyes. He put the uneaten halves of the cookie on the side of the plate. Carson held a fresh cookie out to him. "Cookie?"

Hades felt spit gather in his mouth. Tempted by a cookie, it bordered on the ridiculous. He felt like the Devil held out his hand, beckoning.

"Thanks, no, I had one already. Nice to meet you." Hades rose to refill his coffee. He could live forever on caffeine and had, at points in his life. This Carson Smith was dangerous. His body knew it even if his mind couldn't wrap itself around the shiny wrapper.

# Chapter Three

"What the hell are you trying to pull, Xavier?" The angry call was unwelcome but not unexpected. Father Xavier had prayed it wouldn't come. Sometimes, prayer wasn't the answer. At least God had spared him a personal visit

"How nice to hear from you. What's the matter?" A thin bead of sweat formed on his top lip.

"I asked for a preacher for my sister. She says you sent some hermit with robes and sandals who smells."

"It wasn't my decision. We don't have any priests available. The assignment came from much higher up. Friar Hades is a devout and religious man." Damn, Hades. Why couldn't he be more likeable?

"I gave four million dollars to your building fund last year and I can't get a lousy priest for my sister? Are you shitting me?" The man's voice went up like a cat scratching a pipe.

"I did the best I could! No one is going into the priesthood anymore. Only the largest, most lucrative cities can get a priest. Only by the grace of God himself was I able to get her anyone remotely suitable." Father Xavier's hands blanched as they clutched the chair.

"Some crazy man? How is that helping? Fell's not a very forgiving place. Those people work hard and want their religion on Sunday just like they want their football. You'll be lucky if they don't lynch him. Just pray he doesn't go over the time limit for his sermon or they might be a revolt."

"He's a good man," Xavier regained some of his composure. "He's a true believer."

"What did he do? You're dumping him out in BumbleFuck, he must have done something to embarrass you guys. He better not be a pedophile. I'll shut you guys down if you sent one of those child fuckers to my sister."

"No, I would never. How can you even say that? He's unusual, that's all. He's only been there a few days, give it some time. Has he done anything wrong?" Xavier held his breath.

"I'll give it a month and if I'm not hearing great things; you pull this jerk."

"I can't guarantee you'll get a replacement."

"Maybe the Episcopalians can give me a guy for $4 mill, what do you think?"

"I'll come up with something." he promised. So far Hades had avoided any heinous acts or the man would have been shouting it from the rooftops. It was likely his unsightly looks or perhaps even the screaming night terrors. He needed to get Hades' phone number and keep his finger on the pulse of the situation.


Hades considered himself an excellent judge of men, but women provided a bag full of contradictory messages. Men in foxholes were predictable: they would either curl up in fear, dig deep and do their job or jump out of the hole screaming and charging the enemy. The terror of imminent death exposed the raw kernel of humanity in each man. So, in his heart of hearts, the part that understood things at the animal level, he knew this Carson was evil.

When he got his coffee, blistering hot in the thin white Styrofoam cup, he found his chair occupied by a large woman with a Moe-Curly-Larry haircut. Her thighs spilled over the sides of the chair. Carson had disappeared.

He stood undecided about where to go. He was awful at social crap. Like Moses parting the sea, people streamed around him, maneuvering out of his way. He took a sip. Damn it was good coffee, but so hot, it threatened to melt the Styrofoam. He could drink about six of these before the acid brew became a fireball in his stomach.

"Are you having fun, yet?" Carolyn Bennington smiled up at him. Her smile indicated she knew exactly how uncomfortable he was.

"I feel like a shark in the ocean. Everyone just glides out of my way. I'm not good at this chit-chat stuff."

"You need to have talking points. I think you scared everyone with your, 'I'm watching you' sermon. It wasn't bad for a first effort though. Plus, I think we could all use some watching."

"What are talking points?" If his flock wouldn't even speak to him, it would be hard going helping them. About 80 people filled the small basement. He estimated double had attended the sermon. Some of it was due to people wanting to see the new guy but some of it was lack of anything else to do in Fell, he reasoned.

"Do you know anything about football?"

"Ah, just what any guy knows. I played a little."

"You aren't a Viking's fan, are you?" She scowled at him, brows knit together into an unforgiving white line.

"Not really a fan at all."

"Well, you need to become a Packer's fan, rabid if possible. That's the fastest way to this crowd's heart, everyone is a Packer Backer, except for Ben Weston, he's a Bears fan. Most just ignore him on game day. Oh, and you should be able to speak about quarrying stone."

"Is that the major industry around here?"

"Boy, they didn't brief you at all, did they?"

"No, it was rather sudden, my posting here. What happened to Father Kennedy? You mentioned him before."

"He drank himself to death, bourbon, mostly. Nobody minded as long as he wasn't falling down drunk. He was a quiet drinker but he did go through an amazing amount of liquor on a regular basis. I only know because I did the shopping for him," she confided. "Officially, he had a massive stroke."

"So, Father, I hear you're a runner." A tall man, thin in a short-sleeved green Polo offered his hand for shaking. He pumped Hades' hand with fervor.

"I am. How about those Packers?" He saw Carolyn grimace out of the corner of his eye.

"Mr. Colson is the high school principal," Carolyn put in.

"We sure could use your help. We've got a cross-country team but no one to train them. Mr. Martin read a book on it, but I can't say that he's doing much good. My girl says she saw you running the other day and you were like lightning."

"I'd be happy to help out." He felt the smile pulling at the sides of his face. The damaged skin folded painfully when he smiled.

"They practice right after school each day."

"I'll be there tomorrow. And thanks."

"Are you considered a good runner?" Carolyn smiled at him.

"Yeah, it's great stress relief and you just can't get better cardio." His times pegged him as an elite runner. He had never run much until the army. The army was a big fan of running. They impressed upon him the occasional necessity of saving his fucking hide by being able to haul ass.

He didn't add, he thought football was stupid. All those grown men crashing together getting concussions and damaging their brains. He supposed people said that about running being stupid and pointless too. Every man to his own poison. The all-out effort of running was the best thing for keeping the nightmares at bay, though. Running a lot of miles could be tough on a body. Hades had been lucky that his body was resilient and tough. He'd survived dehydration, heat stroke, a bout with malaria, torture, beatings, extreme temperatures, he'd run the gamut.

"Hades?" Carolyn snapped her fingers in front of his face.

"Sorry, I drifted off." He smiled to apologize. God, all this smiling was painful. His face burned and he hoped it wasn't seeping pus. That was always so attractive. He couldn't even tell when it was happening unless a breeze blew past and he noticed the cooling on his cheek.

"Do that a lot, do you?" She drummed her fingers on the counter in a quick staccato.

An older man, mid 50s Hades judged, with a seamed weathered face clasped one of his hands in both of his. Hades jerked back as the vises closed on him and then tried to relax. Smiling and touching seemed to be the norm in Fell. These people might want more comfort than Hades could possibly give. The things he did for his God.

"Leave the man alone, Carolyn. I drift off a lot too. Wandering, I call it. When I do it, I go someplace better than here. By the look on your face, you go somewhere a lot worse." The older man released his hand and squeezed his shoulder. "Are you a vet, son?"

"Yes, yes, I am."

"Same for me. I saw some terrible things, I can tell you. Where did you serve?"

"Central America, Qatar, Afghanistan, like that. Wherever they told me to go." He hoped the man took the hint and dropped it.

When he stood next to Carolyn, people came to say hello to her and stare at his face. Miss Carolyn provided names and family affiliations. He began to pray fervently that it would end soon.

"Relax, it's just day one. You'll figure it out the lay of the land pretty soon." Carolyn smiled at him.

Was she a psychic? It was one of those scary things that women did.

# Chapter Four

A chill wind swirled around his face, threatening to snatch his breath as he ran the two miles to the high school. The simple rectangular building of tan brick with an angled roof sat at the bottom of a hill. At the sheltered front entrance, a wind sprite picked up leaves and tossed them in a miniature tornado. The morning chill frosted his breath and his muscles weren't warmed up. He could stretch and then run back and forth until the kids showed. He walked to a bike rack and swung one long leg up on it to use it as a stretching bar.

Someone was staring at him. In the triangle between his shoulder blades, tiny hairs stood straight up in a primal warning. Hades learned on the battlefield to listen to his animal instincts. His life had depended upon it many times. He continued his stretch, trying to ascertain the cause of his unease. When he changed legs, he scanned the area to find the source of the gaze.

He jumped when the metal door to the school opened on his left and a group of tall gangly boys edged out. Hades almost smiled because the boys moved as one unit like pack animals did for safety. A trickle of fear rested in his stomach; he had no experience with kids. Their common love of running would have to make the bridge between them so he could connect with them.

They trudged around the side of the school to a crumbling asphalt track, heads down and avoiding his eyes. Hades followed them, intrigued.

The six boys stood at the edge of the track in ill-fitting shorts and t-shirts. Not one of them had the look of a runner about them. Runners should be lean and perpetually hungry with thighs the size of medium trees with odd lobes of overdeveloped muscles hanging off them. These guys looked like they were forced here at gunpoint.

"Hi, guys, I'm Friar Hades. Principal Colson asked me to work out with you." He shook hands with each of them. They each recited their names, with a variety of intonations speaking to their levels of maturity.

Just as quickly as he found out their names, he forgot them. Had he ever been good at remembering names? After his last stint in the desert, there were days and even weeks missing from his memory. His mind never worked the same way after that nightmare as if it were trying to protect him from the worst of it.

"How many miles do you run each week?"

Eyes shifted, one to the other, and finally, the tallest one said, "We mostly run in circles around the track."

"Yeah," put in the smallest boy, "like forever." They all nodded.

Hades waited but nothing more seemed forthcoming. "How many times around each week?"

He could almost feel the gears moving in their heads as they calculated the laps for a week.

"Crap, like eighty or a hundred. Like, I get dizzy sometimes." All the boys giggled.

"So your race is a 5K and you run 20 miles a week? Not enough, gentlemen, not by far. A 5K is five kilometers or three point one miles. For a 5K, you need to put in 40-50 miles a week plus workouts. We'll start today. Let's run twice our race and then we'll do some ladders." The lack of definition in their calves confirmed to Hades that they weren't running over ten miles a week.

They exchanged dark looks and avoided meeting his eyes. Afterwards, he would reflect upon his errors. Not a one of them could run at faster than a seven minute per mile pace. Hades could hardly go slow enough to keep pace with them. When they began to walk the fourth mile, he turned them around.

They straggled back to the school and he had them do 20 push-ups and assorted fitness exercises. What he found distressed him. They had to increase their fitness before they could increase their mileage. Core strength was a huge part of running success, that and base miles.

He left them exhausted but he didn't know who was more depressed: him or them. He gave them a little pep talk at the end and hoped they showed up tomorrow. The worst part was that he didn't even get a decent workout running with them and would have to run again later. The two miles to the high school and back was barely a warm-up for Hades. He enjoyed high mileage running, often a hundred miles a week. Fortunately, he was tough, stringy and durable enough to stay injury free. Running from the pavement onto the gravel of the drive, Hades slowed to a walk to save wear and tear on his shoes. They used large diameter gravel here in Wisconsin, damned near boulders. With a quarry not a mile down the road, you'd think they could do better.

Passing through the tiny porch into his rooms, something made him stop. He found a letter. It was on the seat of the chair he had put outside to write his sermon. Someone walking past the cabin wouldn't see it although Hades doubted much foot traffic went past. The cabin was set at least five hundred feet back from the road. It was further hidden by the large rectangle of the church. Hades exerted all his self-control and ignored it as if going inside to grab a drink. From the kitchen window, he stilled himself, alert to any movement in case someone was watching to see him pick up the card. After ten minutes, he went out and picked it up and came inside. He got some water in a glass and went outside again, still in his shorts and t-shirt.

The envelope was a standard business envelope available anywhere. Inside was a sheet of notebook paper.

It said: "They killed the last preacher. They'll kill you too."

Hades turned it over and then went and got a plastic bag and put the envelope and letter in it. He guessed he should call the police. Or should he?

If someone killed the priest, the police ought to know about it. He sighed. He had a fleeting vision of Father Xavier's displeasure. If this letter writing asshole expected Hades to run, a grim smile touched his face, half of it a horrible grimace. The killer, if there was one, had no idea who he was up against.

But right now he needed information and the best place to start was the police.

He found the phone and made a call. The dispatcher promised to send out the Sheriff as soon as he got back from having pie. She offered to go get him if it was urgent but Hades said it could wait till the man finished his pie. Getting use to the slower pace in Fell would take some doing.

It gave Hades time to wash up and don his robe. He needed protein after his run and inhaled a piece of cheese and a beer while he waited. Who would want to kill a priest, especially a drunk, if that part was true? Someone who wanted to deny people their God.

A righteous anger welled up inside him. His vision became tinged with red and his hands closed spasmodically. And then a cool calm washed over him. He recognized it as the calm he always got before battle was joined. Everything slowed and his vision got sharper. Colors clearer. His whole being relaxed with the prospect of mayhem and he smiled a truly terrible smile.

# Chapter Five

The crunch of gravel alerted Hades to the arrival of the Sheriff. He appreciated the hills that funneled the echo, bring the sound to him: no one would be able to sneak up on him. Hades shook his head to dislodge the war-like thoughts and went out to the porch with the letter and two beers. Tactics and defensive positions had no place in this little town or in his life as a soldier of God.

The battered, dark blue Suburban didn't slow as it rumbled past the church and approached the cabin. Hades barely controlled his urge to dive out of the way. The Sheriff hit the brakes about ten feet from the porch and the big V8 coughed and stopped when the dented front bumper nudged the railing of the porch. No wonder the porch was in disrepair.

The metal of the door groaned and the Sheriff got out and slammed the big door shut with a rattle of rusted. The Sheriff, a tall, spare man of about forty ambled over, in no particular hurry.

"Thanks for coming, Sheriff." Hades extended his hand.

"No problem. You settling in all right? Seems you 'bout ran the legs off the running boys."

"News travels fast here," he handed over the letter in a plastic bag.

"No secrets in this town," laughed the Sheriff.

"We finished our run not a half hour ago. How could you have heard it so fast?"

"Well, let's see, one of your runners got picked up by his mom and they came to the diner where I was having some pie. Then, Helen, the dispatcher told me you asked to see me out here about some letter. And here I am."

The Sheriff took out cheap reading glasses and looked at the letter through the plastic.

"Priest wasn't murdered. He drank himself to death." He muttered and sat down in Hades' chair, putting his boots up on the railing of the porch. The Sheriff accepted a beer. His uniform was dark brown, exclusive of ornamentation except his badge. He didn't wear a holster, although Hades could see a shot gun standing straight up in the front of the truck.

"Was there an autopsy?" Hades sat on a porch rail, drinking his beer, trying to stay upwind of the man, out of habit.

"Of course, we're not the backwater you've been led to believe." He smiled at Hades to take the sting out of his words. His uniform was neatly pressed, simple without any ornamentation. He wasn't wearing handcuffs or any of the forty-five pounds of gear patrolmen wore in New York.

"Well the letter made me wonder who'd want to throw a scare into me."

"Pardon my frankness, Friar, but for all the robes and shit you don't look like a man who scares easily. I heard you put the fear of God into the congregation yesterday." He chuckled and it dissolved into a wet coughing fit.

"Well, I wouldn't go that far," Hades said although he was pleased.

"I might even start going to church again, who knows? Miracles can happen even in Fell." He slugged down the rest of the beer and left the can on the railing.

"I hope you do. I'll look for you. I might even do a sermon on law enforcement if I was sure you were going to attend." Hades regretted the words as soon as they left his mouth. Sermons on request? Specific topics? Just because he had survived one Sunday without falling on his face, didn't mean he was an expert. It gave him a new respect for those men of the cloth who preached week in and week out.

The Sheriff drove off and Hades took the empty cans inside. Maybe he would wash them out and save them for target practice. Wait, he didn't have a gun. A smile graced his face; could he put that on his grocery list? What would Miss Carolyn say about that?

The phone rang. Wasn't he the popular one? It took him half a minute to find where he'd left it. Miss Carolyn had given him the cell phone that had been Father Kennedy's. Hades guessed it made sense for him to have a communication link in case there was an emergency.

"Friar Hades."

"Ah, Hades, this is Father Xavier. How's it going?" Hades pictured the good-looking priest and wondered why he'd called. Certainly not to see how Hades was doing.

"Fine. I gave my first sermon on Sunday."

"Sermon? Ah, yes, you're filling in for the priest that died."

"I have a new respect for preachers."

"Oh, well, they don't make it up every week. There's a bulletin that comes out. Here let me make a note for my secretary to add you to the list. It gives you a prepared sermon with hymns and verses and your homily. I'll make sure you're on the mailings. What I really wanted to talk about is how things are going."

"Things are going well. I got my first death threat today."

"Death threat? No, Hades, not acceptable!"

"Just a letter. Implied that the previous priest had been killed. I spoke to the Sheriff but he says Father Kennedy drank himself to death."

"Well, if he says it was an accident, it was. Hades, I really need you to get along with the people down there. There's some pressure from powerful donors. They wanted a priest but all we had was you."

"Makes me feel all warm and fuzzy." Hades looked with longing at the refrigerator where the beer was kept.

"Listen to me! We need you to succeed in Fell. Can't you be a little bit more lovable? More respectable? More like people's vision of a holy person?" His voice went up as he got more exasperated.

"Listen, I'm sorry I'm not anyone's idea of a priest. I'm a Friar. I need to be in New York where I fit in better, not this sleepy little white bread community of judgmental snobs." He moved to hang up, thought better of it and took a deep breath.

"I'll try Father, that's all I can promise. I'll try to be what these people need."

"Hades, try to be what I need. I need you to fit in down there. Make those people like you. Consider it a direct order from God." Father Xavier hung up the phone.

"Make people like me?" Hades shook his head. Saving souls wasn't a popularity contest. If it was, he wasn't going to be very good at it.

# Chapter Six

"I really, really like him." Carson said out loud. He conversed with himself often. He preferred to associate with intelligent people and so he spent quite a lot of time alone. "I'd like to be best buddies, but how do I do that? Perhaps I'll arrange a welcome to Fell event." He rummaged in his father's closet till he found what he wanted: black pants, shirt and a black knit cap. There was gasoline in the garage by the mower. He waited till it was solid dark and took his supplies three streets over where the town's only gay couple lived.

The two men kept to themselves and bothered no one. They'd be the perfect welcome for the Friar. It was going to be so exciting to have him around. Carson had considered leaving Fell for greener pastures. His father might retaliate but the boredom was excruciating. He hated being bored. The Friar would be a nice diversion. Weren't holy men just made for tormenting? It was practically in their job description.

He spread the gasoline around the foundation of the garage on the side away from the house to make sure they wouldn't notice the smell. The running shoes on his feet were a size too large but the best he could come up with short of buying some. The soft mud made a clear print. Was it too perfect? He considered and smudged it. Too bad he didn't know the Friar's size. The man was coaching cross-country at the local high school. What a loser do-gooder. Or perhaps he had a thing for little boys. Just spreading such a rumor might be enough to ruin the good man.

He laid a trail of gasoline away from the garage; far enough so he could light it without burning himself. He took one last look around and struck the match. The soft whomp made him move back a few steps. The almost invisible flames raced along the line of gas he'd left and licked at the garage. Time to leave.

He backed away. It was too bad the Friar lived in such an out of the way place. He would love to leave the gas cans in his backyard. He put the cans away in his own garage and the shoes under the back seat of his car. Disposal could wait till tomorrow in the river.

"Miss Carolyn, I need your help." Hades strode into the church office the next morning after his conversation with Xavier. He might not understand the tall, dignified priest, but he respected his ability to get along.

The woman was always neat and put together. Today, she had on a pink sweater and dark slacks. It probably drove her nuts that he was a mess. Hades rubbed the quarter inch stubble on his head. It itched like crazy and he rubbed it to stop from itching. He forced his hands to his sides. Wouldn't do to add scabs on top of his already lovely face.

"What can I do for you, Friar?" She rolled back her chair and frowned at him. He wasn't sure she liked him. Was she judging him in the harsh light of Father Kennedy? Hades had written down a list yesterday after speaking to Father Xavier. After swearing creatively for a time, he prayed. Peace and obedience settled about him like a mantle. He needed a plan. Item number one on the list was enlisting Miss Carolyn as an ally. People liked her and respected her. When he was with Miss Carolyn, people came up and spoke to him.

"I need to be more likable. I need to be a part of this town. Can you help me?" He plopped into the wooden chair in front of her desk.

She stared at him with her mouth open.

"I get the feeling you don't like me. I know I'm kind of a wreck to look at but I have nothing but the best intentions. My mission is to bring souls to God. Every moment I sit here; there are souls I could save, but I figure I have to start with you. Everyone seems to respect you in this town; I could see it at the church in the basement. So, help me out, how do I change?"

"Well, it's not that I don't like you, Friar." She began.

"Then, you like me?" He felt like an eager puppy.

"Well, it's not that either."

"So, you don't like me."

"Let me finish! It isn't you, per se. We had a priest, he wasn't the best. You might have heard that he imbibed, but he was a real priest. He died and we were all hoping, well mostly me, that we'd get a priest to replace him. Instead, we got you. Not that you aren't fine, but you don't preach, you can't marry people, you can't baptize." She counted off his flaws on her fingers.

"Hold on! I can do all those things. I just haven't been called upon to do them. My first sermon went ok."

"It wasn't bad," she conceded. "A little on the scary side."

"So, will you give me a chance?" She was the key. If she accepted him, everyone else would fall under his dubious charm.

"Well, start by having coffee downtown every morning."

"I have coffee at home every morning."

"But, if you had coffee downtown at the coffee shop, you would see half the town there coming and going. They could get use to you." she sorted some papers on her desk, not meeting his eyes.

"Ok, coffee downtown every morning. What will I talk about to them? I know you won't believe this: but I am not the world's best conversationalist." He confided.

She fought it but the laugh slipped out. "Yeah, I get that. Ask about the weather, the Green Bay Packers, ask what they want you to preach about. Ask them what are the most pressing problems of the town. That will generate some heated debate if not an outright fist fight. Plus, you'll get all the news about what's going on in Fell and the surrounding communities."

Hades pulled a notepad over and made notes.

And so the next morning, he was hearing about the fire from two volunteer firefighters who had stopped in to gossip.

"It was definitely arson. The report isn't out yet, but I've been fighting fires long enough to recognize the scent of gasoline," Don Plano said. Hades found out the man also doubled as the fire chief in addition to being the quarry foreman.

"Do you see a lot of arson around here?" Friar Hades asked. He was getting the hang of keeping the conversation rolling.

"Naw, not since Jackson went up for burning down his parents' house. They died. Lucky those two guys didn't buy it last night."

"They got out because one of them wasn't feeling well and couldn't sleep. He smelled the gas and they got out. Real lucky. Someone doesn't like them living here in Fell."

"Why would someone not like them living here?" Friar Hades asked.

"They're gay boys. Unnatural, I say, but if they pay their taxes and they don't walk around wearing feather boas, who cares? They root for the Packers, just like all the normal folk around here."

"So you think someone targeted them because they're gay?"

Plano shrugged. "They found some footprints, gym shoes. Be nice if they found the fella who wore 'em. I say lynching's too good for him. Not just for taking that whole house to ashes, but putting everyone fighting the fire, their lives in danger plus other homes near it. It's just an awful thing, fire is. I can see you understand what I'm talking about, Friar."

Hades nodded even though the damage to his face was done by acid, not fire. It was much the same vicious pain from what he knew. He wouldn't wish it on anyone. He could still feel the burning somewhere deep on his nerve endings. The itching was the worst part or was it the sensitivity to temperature? Hard to say.

The Sheriff walked in, nodded and got his coffee. Hades liked that they didn't serve all sorts of designer coffee here. He got the impression cream was looked upon as a weakness of character.

"Take a walk with me, Friar."

Hades picked up his coffee and followed the Sheriff out the swinging door.

"Found some gym shoe prints at the scene. Mind telling me what size shoe you wear?"

"Ten and a half."

"Don't get that look on your face, I'll be checking everyone's shoe size. You're the new guy, so I'm checking you first. Plus, you've been seen wearing gym shoes."

"Scandalous."

"Sarcasm won't get you on my good side, son. I don't believe you did it, but together with that letter you got, I'm worried someone is focusing attention on you and not in a good way. Where were you last night around 2am?"

"Praying. I often have trouble sleeping so I either run or pray depending on which might do the most good."

"Run at night?" The Sheriff recoiled.

"Is that a problem?" Hades could feel a hard edge come into his voice.

"Not for the wolves and occasional cougar. You're skin and bones but as fast as you run, some wild things might take it as a challenge to hunt you down. And I'm not just talking about the humans in these parts." He drank the steaming coffee. Hades grimaced. He drank it like it was the temperature of milk.

"Shit, you've got to be burning the hell out of your throat! I've been here an hour and my coffee's still too hot to drink."

"Years of practice, Friar." The old coot almost smiled.

"I understand you have to do your job, but I can tell you that fire would be the last thing I'd ever be around. For one thing, it hurts like hell. The scar tissue on my face is still sensitive years later. I can't take cold and heat bothers me too. Fire, no way." Hades shook his head. He had gotten some cream to desensitize it at the VA hospital but when it ran out, he hadn't bothered to get it filled. Maybe he should reconsider. The winters were most likely brutal here in Northern Wisconsin.

The thought of his face drying and cracking made him grimace.

"Got an idea?" The Sheriff scrutinized him.

"Just how cold does it get here?"

"On average in the winter, I'd say the temperature hovers just below zero. We can get some hellacious cold wind though knocking the temp down to double digits below."

"Man, that's cold. Is there a VA hospital near here? I probably should get some cream for my skin." He remembered one time it had cracked; the bleeding had been impossible to stop.

"One about twenty miles from here. Hitch a ride with Miss Carolyn when she does her shopping. Every week or so she goes over there for whatever."

"Thanks I appreciate it."

"Always happy to help a fellow vet. Air Force, myself."

"Chair Force? I was a recon scout with the army."

"Whatever, asshole," but the Sheriff smiled and nodded. "Let me know if you see anything suspicious on those night runs of yours, and don't let all those glowing eyes worry you," the Sheriff laughed as he walked off.

The Sheriff might seem buddy-buddy but that didn't fool Hades. He had run afoul of enough military police to realize the man's antennae were vibrating. Hades was the new factor in town. Therefore he had to be evaluated and judged. Shit he didn't need this and went back to try his coffee again. Damn, it was still scalding.

# Chapter Seven

"Miss Carolyn, next time you head to Trent, could I tag along? I want to stop in at the VA hospital."

"I can go tomorrow, if you like. You need to make me a grocery list."

Crap. What did he need to survive? Peanut butter, beer, beans? He was used to eating at soup kitchens in New York. He had no idea how to cook. He bent down and wrote his meager needs on a scrap of paper.

Miss Carolyn looked at it and frowned. She added: vegetables, deodorant, shampoo, soap. "What do you eat for breakfast?"

"Coffee." His gut was churning from the harsh brew down at the coffee shop and gurgled audibly.

Miss Carolyn shook her head. "If you're going to hang with the pros, you need to eat something before you drink that stuff. It's like you wouldn't go drinking without a base of food, right? How about a muffin?"

"A muffin." He mulled it over. It seemed a frivolous piece of food for a Friar. He couldn't picture St. Francis of Assisi pulling out a muffin in the morning so he could drink a gallon of java without distress.

"No butter or jam, that ought to make it severe enough for you. You probably need a good 3500 calories a day if you're going to run every day." She added muffins to the list. "What about lunch?"

"I'm not really that into eating. In New York, I just did whatever the street people did. Ate what they ate."

"Well, there aren't any street people in Fell. Not too many miss a meal at all, if you take my meaning. If you want to fit in, make a connection with this population, eating is key. We eat and we eat a lot. All celebrations focus around food."

"I'm not anti food, I just don't know how to cook. I'm supposed to be focused on the soul."

"If you faint from hunger, people here are just going to step over you to get to the buffet line. No one is going to be impressed, your holiness. There's a schedule for home visits on your desk."

She looked down and scribbled a few more items. Hades knew a dismissal when he saw one. He went to pee again. Another downside of drinking so much coffee, is he had to evacuate it every 20 minutes for the next couple of hours. Was it his imagination, or was his urine hotter than normal?

He went into his office which he noted was a third the size of Miss Carolyn's and without a window. It had a battered wooden desk and three hard backed wooden chairs. The room was painted a dismal dark green. Would Miss Carolyn let him paint it? He saw the neatly typed list. There were three names, addresses, plus a two line synopsis of why he needed to visit.

"Petri Thomas, 79, broken hip, bored.

Annabel Fellows, 88, arthritis, wants to get a good look at new Friar.

James Cannon, 56, stage four cancer, won't go to hospice."

Looked like a depressing afternoon. No wonder Father Kennedy had been a drunk. He was hoping the package from New York with the sermons would come before Sunday. He better work on something, just in case.

Hades listed some possible topics: the fire, gays, world peace, shit. He hated this stuff.

"Here are the keys to the truck. You can keep them." Miss Carolyn lobbed them at him. He caught them and went to inspect his new ride. It had been years since he'd driven.

It was a classic Bronco from the 90s. Four-wheel drive, almost mint. The inside was spotless and the mileage was low. It was awesome. Much like he appreciated the way his rifle fit together and was exceptionally good at its function, he appreciated the big V8. The Bronco was white and the tires looked new. He went back in and got his list of shut ins and was happy to note that there was an aftermarket GPS. He punched in the address of Petri Thomas and put the big beast in reverse.

Thomas' was easy to get to, just off Main Street. Hades wondered if he should have brought anything. He knocked on the front door.

"Well, come in. I'm sure not coming to you."

The tiny house was neat as a pin. He saw Petri on the couch with her remote close at hand. The couch looked like it doubled as her bed while her hip was healing. A sturdy four post walker stood next to her.

"Well, so you're the new guy, huh?" Alert eyes in a wrinkled face appraised him. A cap of tight gray curls covered her head and she grabbed her glasses off the side table.

"I'm Friar Hades. Pleased to meet you Ms. Thomas." He stood awkwardly wondering if he should take a seat.

The old woman chewed on her lip for a minute, distracted by something out of his sight and then yelled, "Baskervilles. What is Baskervilles?" He realized she was watching Jeopardy.

"I used to teach school. Use those game shows to keep my mind sharp. Don't try to put anything over on me, young man. I've seen it all." She pointed a bent finger at him. "Want some coffee? You're lucky I have any left. Next time, call before you just show up. What if I was naked?" She cackled and wheezed, holding her side. "Now look what you made me do! I have to go pee."

She pushed herself up using her hands on her knees and then grabbed the walker. Hades thought about helping her but didn't want to get chewed out again. All these folk seemed self-sufficient and proud of it.

Petri made her way in starts and jerks across the scored parquet floor to the hallway. She didn't bother to close the door. Her walker wouldn't fit into the bathroom with the door closed.

Hades cringed at the grunts of pain and labored breathing. God, it was tough getting older. He could see it even running. He didn't used to warm up at all; now, he risked pulling something if he didn't do a proper warm up and afterward, stretch.

He listened for the water to run indicating she'd washed her hands. He recited a psalm as she struggled back to the couch. .

"So, you're a Friar eh?"

"Yes."

"What's the difference between a Friar and a priest?" She fell back into the couch in a controlled slide.

His spine straightened like it was an oral exam from the Friary. "Well, a Friar is more responsible for a wider geographic area. We can do weddings and baptisms and preach but generally we don't."

"How come we can't get a priest? Can you deliver the holy sacraments?"

"There just aren't a lot of priests available. I think they go to the richer places. And yes, I can do the water and wine."

"Fuckin' bunch of pedophiles is what they are. Are you normal?" She peered at him.

"Normal? Probably not," Hades admitted. The small woman laughed.

"Don't, I'll have to pee again and it hurts to move around. I was surprised Miss Carolyn didn't have enough pull to get us a priest."

"What does she have to do with it?" Rather than disclose what might be a confidence, Hades played dumb.

"Her brother gives millions to the diocese in New York, way I hear it. She told everyone she was going to ask him to put in the good word. Guess it didn't quite work out. You're a sorry excuse for a priest. Are you going to tell me what happened to your face or will you force me to listen to gossip?"

"I was a soldier before I became a Friar. Some Al-Qaeda assholes dripped acid on my face. It may have been just hours or for days, I have no way of knowing. After the pain hits a certain point, everything kind of blurs out."

"Know what you mean. I won't take those damn pain pills. In the amount of time I've got left, I want to BE there." She pounded the couch arm.

"You're tougher than me," he laughed. "I gladly would have taken anything to stop the pain." He flashed on beating the two men with a chair leg. He'd broken his hand to get out of the bonds so he could only hit with one arm. Blood had splashed up at him for some time before the realization came that they were dead and he could run.

"I like you, Friar. You don't bullshit me. You don't know how refreshing that is at my age, especially after teaching so many years. Here, go grab a cup of coffee, I got plenty. Did you see that last Packer game? Their defense sucks. I'd like to see them use the tight ends more, old school like."

They chatted about football, his part of the conversation non-committal. He only hoped she didn't make him go get more coffee.

"You don't know shit about football, do you?"

"I played in high school but I'm more of a runner."

"Well, start watching. Come into town and watch it with me. We'll tailgate a little even. I'll teach you what you need to know to fit in around here."

As he followed the directions to Annabel Fellows' house, he smiled. He had enjoyed Petri's wit. He told her he would come by for the game and bring beer. She was going to supply the brats. He was intrigued. He had never had a brat. Ditto cheese curds. They sounded dreadful.

When he left, Petri was on the phone ordering brats and cheese curds for Sunday delivery. When he hemmed and hawed about attending, she told him the whole town would shut down anyway and if he wasn't watching the game, people would instinctively dislike him. Half an hour and she could already read him like an expert tracker.

Likewise, she had directed him into her bedroom to get a shirt he was to wear on game day. He balked but she argued he didn't wear his robe running and wearing a green and gold jersey was essential to the experience. He knew he was on shaky theological ground and took the jersey. He would have to wear it with his shorts or buy something to wear with it. Maybe sweats? They would serve double duty when he ran in the winter as warm-ups.

The name on the back was Brett Favre. He recognized the name. Even though he hadn't played since high school, some part of his brain noted the waxing and waning of teams and quarterbacks in the NFL. He wasn't the current quarter back but Petri assured him it was still acceptable to wear the jersey around town, should he choose, and he better choose if he wanted to hang with her.

He pulled into the Fellows' drive and narrowed his eyes. Every square inch of the small front yard was covered in gnomes, plastic flamingos, and painted plywood garden shit. The house itself was purple. If any house had burned to the ground, he thought uncharitably, it should have been this one.

He pushed the button and a cartoon tune played instead of a bell. Serious whack job, he thought. He'd met some in the army. They seemed to gravitate toward recon positions, like they had a death wish. Some believed they were justified in doing anything to anyone they came upon: friendly or not. It angered him. Some of the commanders looked the other way. Good scouts and forward position men were hard to come by. If there was a little collateral damage, well so be it. War was a bitch. Hades didn't agree.

The door opened by itself. It wasn't until he looked down that he saw her. Four foot two, eyes like lasers in her wrinkly little apple doll head. She had wispy fine hair of silver and he could see her red scalp peeking through. There was something infinitely worse about bald women than bald men, he thought. Just unnatural. Her bright pink lipstick trailed down to her chin. If it had been red, he would have suspected zombies.

"Hello, I'm Friar Hades."

She looked at him so long that he worried she might refuse him entry.

She shook her head and sighed. Still she didn't open the door, simply turned and walked away, leaving it ajar. She didn't look like she had arthritis. She had the vacant look of some of the street people he'd known.

Finally, Hades pushed open the door and followed.

She turned into a room on the left and he trailed behind her.

"Mrs. Fellows?" He called.

"It's Miss, please and thank you!" The mirror image of the woman at the door was sitting in a big pink canopy bed. Not just pink, but pink in capital letters. The sheets and bedspread were pink as well as the walls including the ceiling, the drapes were pink and the 70s era shag rug was a faded pink.

Hades didn't know how long he could stay in the room. It seemed to vibrate and he thought his brain might start to throb soon. It made it hard to focus on the little woman and her doppelgänger.

"I'm sorry, I missed what you said."

"Pull the cotton out of your ears. What the hell happened to your face?"

She had propped herself up with a raft of pink pillows. Her silent twin was sitting in a small pink chair that looked like the legs had been poorly sawed off.

"I was a soldier and some not so nice men burned my face with acid."

"Like torture?"

"Exactly like torture."

"Well, I suppose if you survived that, you can survive Fell. You like football?"

It seemed the room held its collective breath. "I played in high school. Being in Friar school, I've been away from the world so I need to get back into it." It wasn't exactly a lie. It seemed like the town revolved around football and coffee.

The twins looked at each other and nodded. The one sitting in the chair got up and went to the pink painted closet. She took a pink baseball cap with what Hades recognized as the Green Bay Packer logo on it and reformed the brim carefully.

He held out his hand and the twin smiled and handed it reverently to him. There was a mirror on the vanity and he set the hat carefully on his head and squatted to look at himself.

Did God always require sacrifice? He noted he needed to do a better job shaving. Of course, no hair grew on the scar tissue but the other side of his skin had a fine mat of stubble. He attempted a smile but it just wouldn't come.

"Thank you."

"It's pink to support breast cancer awareness."

Was it ok for a guy to wear pink around here? They seemed a pretty rough and tumble lot. He wasn't worried he would get beat up; he could hold his own against anyone. He was worried about being liked.

She pointed at another small pink chair with the legs sawn off and he sat. He could barely see over the edge of the raised canopy bed. His knees were as high as his chest.

"Emily, get the man some coffee." The little woman left without comment.

He was on the verge of saying no but he heard Father Xavier's voice admonishing him to be likable. He was worried about the state of the lining of his stomach. He wasn't sure it could survive living in Fell, Wisconsin for any length of time.

"Emily is a few short of a deck, Friar," Annabel confided in him. "She doesn't speak much. Something happened to the cord on the way out. We take care of each other."

Then, the small woman was back with more coffee. She stood in front of him and watched him intently as he took a sip. No one in this town even asked if he wanted cream.

"Wonderful." The already tender skin on the roof of his mouth sloughed off one side as the scalding coffee hit it. He played with the skin that dangled for an hour and listened to the intricacies of rheumatoid arthritis. He nodded at the right places and asked questions where he could come up with them.

He escaped into the Bronco while there was still light in the sky. Should he try to see the last person on the list? He checked his list. Stage four cancer deserved a visit. James Cannon.

He put the Bronco in reverse, happy with the growl of the V8. His mouth would heal eventually.

James Cannon lived in a rugged modest bungalow with a neat yard. Hades knocked on the front door. A blur of white and gray came barreling around the side of the house, digging huge clumps of sod as it came for him and growling in a register so low the hair on his back stood up. Panic had never frozen him; he was one of those rare individuals who could make split second decisions as he was moving. It was one of the things that made him such a perfect and deadly soldier.

He stepped on the top rail of the decorative fence near the front door and propelled himself onto the roof of the ranch using the gutter. There was a moment when his heart stopped beating as the gutter screamed and began to tear off the roof, but then he was safe. The dog or wolf or whatever the fuck it was must have gone 120 pounds. It got a good four feet of air as it tried for him, snapping and growling.

Hades wondered what Father Xavier would say if he saw his Friar trapped on the roof by a dog. A high whistle stopped the dog and he lay down, head between his paws. His yellow eyes never left Hades.

A flannel shirt came around the house first. Hades had a nice view of the man's head sparse white hair covered a shiny pink scalp.

He looked first at the dog and then up at Hades.

"You're a nimble one, aren't you?" He laughed and went back around the house. He reappeared with a ladder.

Hades kept one eye on the dog and the other on the rungs as he climbed down.

"Thanks. I thought he had me." He negotiated the rungs easily despite his robe.

"She. Greta."

"She's huge for a female." Greta wagged her tail at him and then permitted her head to be scratched.

"Yup, part wolf, some say all wolf. She doesn't always obey, has her own mind about things. She probably wouldn't have hurt you; she just likes to see people run and scream. Always wanted to mate her but didn't like the guys who came around. The owners were bigger dicks than the dogs. Pardon my French." He shook his head as they walked to the back of the house. Hades liked the sound of the leaves rustling against the hem of his robe.

"Where did you get her?" Weren't wolf hybrids illegal?

"Found her as a pup a few years ago when I still walked a lot in the woods. Hand fed her. Sheriff told me I had to get rid of her because she was a wolf but I told him the only way this girl was leaving me was if he shot her." He laughed a short bark. "Sheriff couldn't kill a fly. He got out his gun and she rolled over on her back for a belly pat. He didn't have a chance." They rounded the corner of the house on a small rock path.

Hades exclaimed a soft, "Wow." A redwood deck wrapped around the house and extended into the yard. A small stream wound its way through the back.

"Nice."

"Thanks. I can fish right off the back here. Damn handy with this cancer. I get so weak sometimes." He shook his head and frowned.

Hades would have been content to sit on the porch for the rest of his life.

"Beer or coffee?"

"I would love a beer. I'm about to float away on coffee."

"So, you're a vet." He handed Hades a beer from a cooler and took a seat. Greta fell heavily at his feet.

"Yeah, no secrets in this town, huh?"

"I went coast guard. Thought I'd see the world." He laughed loud and long. Hades laughed too. Coast Guard was one of the most dangerous branches of the military to go into.

"I rode up and down the same stretch of North Carolina coast for four years, getting shot at by drug dealers, fishermen and assorted drunks. I didn't think I'd ever come out alive. Seems like penny ante bitching compared to what you've been through."

"Yeah, sometimes, I can't get it out of my mind. It's like I'm trapped in the memory of this or that. I don't think I'll ever be right, really right." It crystallized for him just this moment. He never would be right. And his mission of saving souls hadn't gone so well yet. Still, he had to give it more time. He'd barely been here a week.

It resonated of failure.

"Don't you worry son, you'll figure out how to deal with it. We all do. Maybe you jumped into this Friar job too quick like. It's not right if you're running away from something. You should be running to something. Then, it's right."

"No, that's one thing I am sure of: God wants me to work for him. I had a vision in the desert." It wasn't something he usually told anyone about. He tried to describe it to the Friar in charge of the decision, the gatekeeper of entry into the order. He had recommended psychiatric counseling to Hades.

Hades was happy to oblige. He'd had counseling after his torture and escape from the camp. He'd be happy to have a few more sessions. He persisted in his quest to be a Friar and had finally succeeded, despite a thick folder of information on him. Conversely, the army kept damned few records of what he'd done and most of that had huge boxes blacked out in case someone got hold of it through the Freedom of Information Act.

"I never was a believer, myself. Though, since they found the cancer this year, there's a comfort settling over me. Ever have that?"

"We call it the 'Peace that Passes Understanding.'" At the lowest point of his torture, when he was in agony, it had come to him, like cool clear water over a burn, a calm, a peace so perfect, he held his breath, lest it slip away. He nodded.

"Why does God let little children get cancer? That's one of the things that has always bothered me. If he notes every sparrow, you'd think he could help some little one in pain."

Greta's ears went on point. She got up and soft footed across the porch. Hades turned to see what she was looking at and startled a squirrel when his head turned. He swore Greta looked at him like he was an idiot.

"I believe that all good comes from God. Those shitholes who tortured me went to the Devil. He seduced them and they were happy to go along and get with his program. They'll be judged in the end." Hades wasn't going to divulge the fact that he had already recycled their souls himself to speed the work along.

"Now little kids with cancer: I believe God gives us these children, the Devil makes them have cancer and then sits back and sees if it's going to break us away from God. Children are a gift. I bet if you talked to the families of the kids, they love those kids; cancer or not. They are happy to have them even for a short while in their lives."

"So God doesn't make people suffer, the Devil does?"

"All the time. It's a war. And every person has to fight their own skirmishes."

"It makes me feel better about God that he's not allowing these kids to suffer."

"The longer I live, the more I believe that everyone suffers. Everyone has scars on their souls from battles won and lost. No one escapes. I just have some of mine on the outside, is all."

"You know Friar, you've brought me some peace. I'll let you get on your way but you've given me something to chew on and I thank you for it. Will you call on me again next week?"

"Absolutely." A cold stab of wet touched his buttocks and he yelped and spun. Greta had nosed under his robes and goosed him.

Cannon dissolved in laughter.

"She did that on purpose!" Hades complained.

"You spooked her squirrel when you moved."

Greta watched him drive off. He could almost swear she was smiling.

# Chapter Eight

The roads were lonely around Fell and Hades fought to keep alert as he drove. The dense firs closed like a curtain along the ridge, although the sun was still in the sky beyond it. He fumbled for the lights, groping blindly on the steering column. He had his lights on or he might not have seen the girl walking on the road ahead of him. He slowed and debated offering her a ride. She was wearing tight, ripped jeans and a long-sleeved form fitting shirt. Her hair was light, probably blond and a gigantic purse hung from her slender shoulder.

His instinct was to stop. At first glance, she was a fellow traveler, a woman alone. But, on second thought, being alone with a woman probably wasn't the safest course for him in any town, much less Fell. Despite the twilight, it was still OK for walking and she wouldn't have started out if it was anywhere too far.

A cabin might sit nestled a hundred feet from the road and he'd never see it. He drove past her, unhappy with his choices. She didn't look his way. The guilt rode with him all the way back to his rooms. He sat in the driveway debating what Jesus would do. He put the big Bronco in reverse and headed back.


"Need a ride?" Carson pulled onto the wrong side of the road so he could be closer to her.

"Are you some kind of stranger danger?" She leaned over so her heavy cleavage rested on the car sill and peered into the dim car.

"Yes, I guess I am," he laughed.

"I know who you are," her voice was seductive and flirtatious. He imagined her practicing it in the family trailer at night while her mom and dad drank themselves senseless.

"Really?" He smiled in the darkness. He loved it when a plan came together. He breathed in the scent of her: unwashed youth and cheap perfume. Intoxicating.

"You're that rich guy, Carson something, your dad owns all the quarries.

"Well, you're smarter than I am because I don't know you, lovely lady."

"I'm Makayla Burnett. I live just down the way in Century Park, but I wouldn't mind going somewhere else either." She put her hand on his thigh. He spared a glance down, it was surprisingly shapely and delicate. Her blond hair was natural. He judged her to be about fifteen. Perfect. It would hardly even be a chore.

If only he had some alcohol. He hadn't known what he was looking to do when he set out to follow the Friar. He needed some kind of transmitter so he wouldn't have to wait on an old logging road while the Friar went on his rounds. He wondered if they sold such things. The time well spent though.

His resolve to play with the man crystallized. The holier than thou thing reminded him so much of his fucking father. His father's idea of a joke; sticking him out here in no man's land to 'watch over' the quarry interest. Just an excuse for shuffling him away from the unfortunate incident in Green Bay. He hated Fell and was determined to make dear old dad pay for tethering him to this small town.

And this little whore fell right into his hands looking for a good time. Well, she would find out they didn't exactly have the same idea of a good time. They were both looking for a way out of Fell. Hers would be an abrupt exit, perhaps but she should thank him. At least she would get out.

Shit! The round headlights of the Bronco crested the hill in front of them, coming directly at his car. What was the Friar doing out again? Would he recognize the Lexus? It was the only one in Fell and crap, it was silver. Was the Friar observant? Was it worth the chance he wasn't?

Damn the man to hell for ruining a good idea. A great plan. A stimulating night of play. The Bronco drove past and turned around a hundred meters down in the wide gravel shoulder.

"Sorry, I can't tonight. I have to see about something." Fucking lame excuse. He pulled away from the little bitch and put his foot to the floor, showering her with gravel, he hoped. He hit the steering wheel in frustration and drove back the way he'd come. He passed the Bronco going the other way and knew his instincts had been spot on. He was a predator and everyone else was prey. The Bronco slowed. The Friar was going back to pick up little miss twat.

As he drove, he considered. What would be the worst thing he could do to the disfigured asshole? Kill him? No, he'd probably like that. Kill someone else? The Friar didn't really know anyone here. But wait, he knew the dick head James Cannon and the hellhound.

The current rumor was Cannon had cancer, stage four. No reprieve. Carson hated the fucking wolf. It had chased him more than once. Somewhere in its animal brain, it saw through him and knew he meant no good. The Friar could be the perfect suspect. No one liked the new kid in town, especially if his face looked like a freak show. People would suspect the Friar of killing Cannon, if just after he visited the dead man to be, the man's only lifeline, the wolf got whacked

It had a certain symmetry to it, plus he would so enjoy killing the animal. How to do it? Poison, he guessed that would work. It was easily attainable in the form of rat poison. He probably could find some at the quarry but that would entail exposing himself. What other options were available?

Shooting? He wasn't that great a shot and it would be traceable. He enjoyed knife work but the beast wouldn't let him within fifty feet of it. Poison it would have to be. Tomorrow, he would drop by the quarry and scrounge around. His fucking father denied him a key or he would go tonight. A nice juicy steak seasoned with rat poison. Cannon would agonize over it. Some people were just too attached to their pets.

It would probably even ease his mind, once he reflected upon it. He wouldn't have to worry who would take the great ugly animal when he died.

And it would cross people's mind that the new Friar had been around. The dog probably hated the Friar like it did practically everyone else. The exception was kids. The animal loved kids. Too bad he couldn't arrange for the animal to kill a kid. Then, the Sheriff would have to put it down.

Too hard to arrange. Besides, his goal was to flush the Friar from the town.

The next morning, he put on his "working man's" clothes as he thought of them. Creased Dockers in dark navy and a starched blue shirt. He wore pristine worker boots and covered it all with a Carhartt jacket. He could slip the poison in its inside pocket.

The air was crystalline clear and so blue it looked fake. The vibrant green of the first contrasted with the changing leaves of the maples. Even the pristine gray of the quarry looked good with the fine layer of gray dust that hung heavy in the air.

He drove the Lexus through the gate and waved at the guard when the man asked him to sign in. He ignored him and saw him on the phone to the office. Damn, that was a bad move on his part. He should have signed in and then he could have gone where he wanted before the foreman was even aware he was there.

The foreman went out to meet him. He wondered if his father left instructions that he be escorted when he was on the quarry premises. Bastard.

"Hello, Carson, what can I do you for today?" The older man wore a plaid shirt tucked into tan dusty work pants. The sun was bright for all it was forty degrees out but the man didn't sport a jacket.

"I thought I'd stop by, get acquainted with the business again. My father..." he shrugged as if to suggest his father wished him to be actively interested in the big hole in the ground.

"Well, he didn't mention it to me this morning." Was the idiot calling him a liar? He got out of the car and shrugged again.

"Mickey, get up to the office, pronto." He spoke into an ear bud. My, weren't things getting high tech at the hole?

An enormous lout was rounding the side of the office. He was moving quickly but slowed when he saw Carson with the boss.

"Carson is going to be tagging along with you today." The big man was Barrington's age and had worked in the hole since he graduated high school.

A pained expression crossed the giant's face, quickly replaced by a forced grin. Carson was hoping he could ditch Mickey. Mickey was covered in the fine dust that all quarry workers came dipped in.

He spent the morning holding tools and going to the bathroom. He refused to use the porta potties, preferring instead to walk all the way back up to the office. Carson pleaded too much coffee drinking this morning.

He seriously slowed down the repair of the machine, whatever the hell it was by his constant interruptions. Yet, every time, Mickey accompanied him to the growing anger of the work crew.

When lunch came, he finally gave it up and left. He wasn't going to get any poison that way. He wanted nothing more than to go home and shower the dust off his body but he resisted. He drove an hour to the next town over, Trent and bought a bunch of different things: wine in a bottle, glasses, rat poison, and duct tape. He went next door to the grocery and got a couple of steaks. He parked the silver Lexus around the side of the building and kept his hat and sunglasses on. He should have done this in the first place instead of wasting his time at the quarry.

He had all the supplies he needed whether he ran into the teenage whore again or the beast in the woods. Could he manage both?

Still, he was unhappy. Neither killing the girl nor the dog provided a direct link to the Friar. He needed to plant some evidence in the house or the church.

If he killed the girl, he could take something and drop it in a pew. The dog was harder to link to the Friar. He could make some gym shoe prints again but that hadn't worked out so well the first time. Oh, well, it would be fun just to kill the dog on its own.

God worked in mysterious ways. He could devise a way to link the Friar after the fact. Rat poison in his house, just a little spilled at the back door, the can buried. Ohh, it felt right. It felt good. He was invincible. He loved the idea of attacking the weak and defenseless holy man in the bullshit robes.

Carson reasoned the girl was coming home from work but from where? Close enough to walk could be from a few steps to two miles around here. He revised his estimate of her age to sixteen, if she was working. He drove back down the road he had seen her on. She was wearing regular clothes so she wasn't a waitress at the diner. It was the only place close enough for someone to walk. It was a tad over a mile over the hilly terrain.

So, it had to be the greasy diner. How eloquent. He pulled in and ordered tea. The waitress looked at him for a second and then went to get his order. She placed the water and a thin tea bag on his plate. Tea in a bag, the heathens. He had his own jasmine tea imported loose. Its fragrance lifted the soul and restored his equilibrium. He would have some when he got home.

A slight film floated on the water and his stomach clenched. A residue of either coffee or soap clinging to the thick white cup. He put the teabag in the steaming water and watched a brown pool expel from it.

There was a cook, a waitress but no other people were visible. If the girl were sixteen, she would still be in school right now. Crap, he should have thought of that.

Coming back at 3:30 was out of the question. Stopping to pretend to drink their disgusting bilge water was permissible once but twice in a day would be remarked upon. Connections might be made.

"Don't see you in here much, Carson." The Sheriff sat next to him. The waitress slid a cup of frothing coffee in front of him while Carson considered which lie to play.

"My dad wants me to spend more time at the quarry."

"Noticed you've got a dusting of real work on you today." The hick stuck a toothpick in his mouth.

"Yeah, it's pretty gross. Not sure I can go back this afternoon. I'll try half days for a while."

"Be good for you to be doing something. Idle hands are the Devil's work."

Carson was going to correct the imbecile. Idle hands were the Devil's workshop but his mouth went dry when he saw her.

She met his eyes briefly and let her eyes slide past him expertly. He liked her panache. She had her ripped jeans and a green t-shirt on with a purple hoodie over it. Shiny earrings hung from her ears and she wore dirty gym shoes. Her bright hair was pulled back into a high ponytail, making her look young and fresh.

"Hey, Makayla, how's it going?" Sheriff nodded at the young woman.

"I'm getting all As." She smiled at the Sheriff and went in back. He could see her through the kitchen pass through.

"Now, there's a survivor," Sheriff said in a quiet voice. "Got a horrible family situation, ma and pa drunks and she's determined to finish her high school diploma and do better. You might take a page from her book, Carson."

She was putting on a white lab coat or such and tucking her hair into a hair net. She was a dishwasher. His gaze fell to his cup and the slight film hovering over the tea. He sipped it and tried to keep his face neutral over the bitterness. He smiled at the Sheriff. The idiot had no idea that Carson meant to take more than a page out of her book.

He left a generous tip and walked out into the cold sunshine. He turned back once and noted the time the diner closed: eight tonight and every night but Sunday. Carson would have to let some time go before he picked her up. Otherwise, the Sheriff might put things together. Even an imbecile can add two plus two.

It was too risky. The Sheriff had seen him there and the girl. He let the plan slip through his mind. He had all the time in the world. Best find another girl.

Hades hovered around the office, checking for the mail. It didn't come until after five in the evening. He prayed that the pre-packaged sermons would come today, sparing him that ordeal, but when the blue truck with the metal US Mail sign on it came up, nothing came for him. He would have to spend his afternoon working up some inspirational words.

He retired to the office and sat at the desk. Procrastination reared its ugly head and he went through the desk drawers. He found a bottle of Jack Daniels and took a swig. It burned down his throat and seared the hairs of his nostrils. He took out a clean piece of paper.

"Let's talk about your soul this week. Are you right with God? Are you walking in Jesus' footsteps?" Was he? Did every step say, "Jesus"? Jesus saved us all from having to walk the terrible path he did. For the millionth time, he pondered on what a tough hombre Jesus must have been.

He dropped and did 100 push-ups. It's what he did when he felt unworthy. He began a second hundred. Jesus had his own Iraq and it was every bit as fucked up as the one Hades knew. Jesus endured torture too and he had a choice and went ahead with it. Given the choice, Hades knew he would have chicken shitted out of the torture in a minute. God give him strength.

"Friar?" Miss Carolyn stood in the doorway, watching him.

He debated continuing, but broke off lest she judge him disrespectful.

"Yes, I'm working on my sermon."

"Obviously. Did you make any visits yesterday? I keep track."

"Yes, I spent time with James Cannon, Ms. Fellows and who was the third one?"

"Petri Thomas? All three?"

"Yeah, Cannon's dog treed me on the roof. He's a great guy. Awesome attitude. Why are you surprised? Did you expect me to play hookey?"

"No. I'm just surprised you jumped right on it."

"It's not like I have a lot to fill up my time with." She stood there and watched him. "I'm working on my sermon."

"I'm certain that you are."

"No really, the push-ups help me reflect. So, far I'm considering calling it, "Walking in Jesus' footsteps."

"Sounds like you're planning another rousing sermon." She smiled at him.

"Too harsh? Should I tone it down? I don't want to offend..."

"Well, since you only have the title, we don't need to worry quite yet. I'll be going into Trent tomorrow if you want to go."

"Yeah I'd love to. I need sweats to go with my new Brett Favre jersey and hat." He held up the jersey and shook it at her. Then he put the hat on his head. "Is it weird for a man to wear pink? I don't want to get beat up."

"Not at all. The Green Bay Packers have a whole group of men who work to benefit breast cancer. You're still manly," she assured him. "Where did you pick up the gear?"

"Well, the Fellows sisters donated the hat and Petri Thomas invited me for brats and cheese curds, whatever they are."

"Tailgating with the locals. Aren't you the social butterfly?"

"I've got to fit in, you said so yourself. I'm following the plan, boss."

She stood in the doorway considering him. "You're different than I first imagined." She turned quickly and walked away.

Was that good or bad. Different how? He wished she elaborated. Should he do more push-ups or was he ready to write?

"The difference between good and bad." He wrote it on the sheet of paper. "Make that good and evil." He rewrote the title.

He pondered the nature of good and evil. To him, it was not as simple as black and white but to God, was it? What would God want him to say about it? The words flowed and he hurried to write them down before the inspiration evaporated. When he was done, two solid pages of writing stared back at him.

The gist of it; the heart of what he tried to say, was there somewhere. He uttered a prayer that he conveyed what his heart held.

When darkness brought a chill, he went inside but couldn't keep still. He fretted from one end of the small cabin to the other and and considered the advisability of running. He pondered the possibility of coyotes and buzzards and such waiting to pick his skeleton clean. There wasn't much meat on his bones. He remembered Greta and the joy she'd found "treeing" him. The night was like the inside of a velvet glove. For all that it was pitch dark, he wanted to run. He walked from the church, back to the cabin and wondered if it was worth twisting an ankle in the darkness.

Hades' night vision was exceptional. It was one of the great gifts that made him such an awesome scout. He'd always taken it for granted, hadn't even realized other people couldn't see in the dark. He treated it like a magician's trick when he was a kid, performing for a crowd of awed onlookers by finding things they named or finding them in a darkened room.

No moon tonight and no streetlights, but if he kept to the road, he wouldn't get lost. He pulled on his shorts and running shoes. A "Nanowrimo" T-shirt completed his outfit. He put the pink Packers' cap on.

He walked to the paved road and did some simple stretches, bounced a few times and headed off for some long slow distance running. If he kept left of the white line, he could keep the road directly ahead of him. He was heading into town, almost to the bridge when the high beams of a car blinded him. It was coming towards him and he took a few steps off the road in case they didn't notice him.

Damn the man to hell! He was everywhere! Here he was, trolling for the cute dishwasher and the Friar is out running. He couldn't believe his bad luck. Or was it good luck? It meant no alibi. Poison the dog right now and turn that frown upside down.

He imagined it slept in the house, probably the same bed as James Cannon. Both probably had fleas. He cut his lights and parked on the same access road stub when he was following the Friar the other day.

He got the steak out of the back and sprinkled the rat poison on it until it was crusted. How close would he have to get to the house to drop the meat for the dog to find it? He'd read somewhere that dogs' sense of smell was forty times that of man.

He certainly didn't want to get close enough that the dog might bark. He had never heard the dog bark but he was sure it would raise the countryside.

The dim lights of Cannon's house flickered through the full woods. He heaved the poisoned steak in the direction of the lights, grunting, then wiping his hands with disgust on a napkin from the car.

Imagine the anguish when dear James whistled and his stupid dog wolf half-breed fucked up monster didn't come. Now might be just the time to bury the poison in the back of the church since the Friar was out on a run. He hurried back to his car and drove to the church. He parked in front of the cabin and ran to put the poison on the side of the church.

If the Friar came back, he could say he came for a visit to check on how he was getting along in Fell. He left the can of poison on the far side of the church where no one would stumble across it accidentally.

Back in his car, he congratulated himself on another phase of his project going forward. He would have the other steak tonight. It was one of the few things he could cook and he did them to perfection. How far did the fucking Friar run? By the time he crossed the bridge, he was sure he would have passed him. No worries, he headed home, content.

Hades did ten miles out at a slow pace and then upped his speed on the way back, completing a full twenty miles. Not bad for a long run. He didn't pass many cars and fewer people. He walked the last hundred feet to the cabin on the gravel drive. He did his full stretch routine and went in for a shower. Hades loved that it was truly dark out here. He had never experienced that in New York City. There was always a red glow from the streetlights at night. It was one of the few things he missed from both the jungles and his time in the desert. Nothing beat laying on a warm sand dune with a light wind on your face and billions of stars overhead. It always brought God closer to him.

He had to admit the daily showering kept his robes cleaner. The wool sucked up all that sweat and kept it like a promise. Plus, the robes took forever to dry when he washed them and hung them to dry.

After his shower, he had run out of things to do. He prayed for about an hour and got up, his knees protesting. He turned down the covers and crawled into bed.

Hades dreaded sleep. Not that it was elusive. He still had the ability to drop into a deep sleep instantly anywhere. He had developed that crucial skill in the army. It was the dreams that chased him nightly. Some nights he relived the days of torture in the desert and others he was beset by bugs covering his body, crawling into dark warm places best left alone. It had been so since the war. He tried to tire himself out by exercise but that didn't work.

And then there were the night terrors. Black soft winged things with sharp claws tore at him until his own screaming woke him. Sweat rolled off him and he shook for hours in abject terror. He believed the things came directly from Hell and were sent to derail his mission to save souls. At times, he tried to go without sleep as long as possible, hoping that would drive the demons away. They came and went as they pleased. Neither denying himself sleep nor getting ample sleep seemed to stem their entry into his nights. The screaming often frightened people and he was glad the cabin was isolated. That was why he had ended up in an unheated cellar room at the rectory in New York. The other priests begged him to seek medical help and he went gladly. He had a sleep test with a dozen wires attached to parts of his body and readings taken constantly but the only thing they could do for him was give him heavy sedatives. They did nothing. He was one of those rare individuals whose body naturally rerouted drugs, rendering most ineffective or giving unexpected results.

He tried the pills but didn't welcome the rampant insomnia that kept him awake for three days and nights. When he finally collapsed he slept for a day and a half and when he did wake it was slowly and without the keen awareness of his surroundings he was accustomed to having. He took them anyway while he was at the rectory. He didn't want people scared of him.

Hades was certain the coffee would prevent sleep tonight. By his count, he'd had in excess of six cups. The very thought made him want to get up and pee. He prayed again for half an hour, prayed for the men he'd killed, each one a vivid bleeding scar on his soul. He went to bed again and dropped off.

In his dream, he was in a choir comprised of all the men he'd killed. They looked like zombies with gaping stab wounds and necks hanging by a thread of a tendon or the back of their heads blown to mist so their faces ended abruptly behind their ears.

They were singing to him and he was tied to the chair where he'd been tortured and they were forcing him to listen. It was painful and he broke his hand to escape like he had in the desert camp.

His eyes came open and he was immediately aware and awake. He replayed the noise in his memory. Car on gravel. He rolled off the bed to a crouch and moved quickly to the side of the front window so he wouldn't be silhouetted.

The vehicle paused a moment and Hades observed the person inside the car heave something out the window towards the church.

Molotov cocktail? He sprinted out of the cabin, front screen banging behind him, but the car was moving fast, spitting gravel behind its wheels. Expecting the worst, Hades looked down and saw the paper. His brain wouldn't process the threat immediately, then he realized there was no threat unless you counted the news.

Crap, if paper delivery was going to wake him up every day, this was going to be a long stint in Purgatory. He sat down and opened the paper to wait for dawn to arrive over the ridge.


When the sky began to lighten, the Sheriff roared up to his cabin. Hades stood up, rather than sit and see if the man ran him over on his own porch. The big Suburban wheeled in a semicircle until the passenger side was towards Hades.

"Get in. There's trouble." The Sheriff called through the open window. Hades climbed into the vehicle which was moving before his butt touched the seat.

Hades was desperate to ask what the trouble was, but he refrained. The Sheriff would explain in his own good time.

They turned into James Cannon's drive and Hades chest dropped. The man must be dead.

The aroma of strong coffee met him as he rounded the house to the spacious porch. James was there and Greta, hackles up looked them over and laid down relaxed at his feet.

"What's going on?" Hades couldn't resist any longer.

"Someone threw some poisoned meat on the property," the Sheriff answered.

"Who would have done such a thing?" Hades asked.

"It looked like it was thrown from somewhere. Do you know anyone who might do something like this?" The Sheriff asked James.

"Some of the farmers have blamed Greta for stealing chickens but they are usually proved wrong when the real culprit comes back for seconds. Of course, I never get an apology," he said bitterly.

"How did you find the meat?" asked Hades.

"I usually come out and get the paper before I make coffee. Greta was waiting for me this morning. Usually she comes out of the woods later when she's done sleeping or whatever. She took me right to it. She knew it was poison."

"What did you bring me here?" Asked Hades of the Sheriff.

"I want you to stay with James while I sort this out. I have some calls to make and some hard questions to ask. I want to make sure he's alright. Poisoning an animal can make it turn on its owner in pain sometimes. I wonder who they were really trying for here?"

"Carolyn's going over to the next town for supplies. Have you got a list?"

"Oh, thanks, I don't need anything right now. I think I'll sit outside for a while. Let Greta chase some squirrels. This whole thing has worried her sick."

Neither the Sheriff or Hades said what they were thinking: that James looked sick, not Greta. They helped get him settled into his chair on the deck.

"James, I'm going to stay with you for a while," Hades drew up a chair.

"I really don't want any company."

"Yeah, tough shit."

"Walk me to the car, Hades." The Sheriff led him around the house.

"How old is Greta?"

"She can't be more than three years old. Seems longer. She was just the thing James needed after he got the cancer the first time. He needed someone to look after to keep his mind off the pain. He didn't go through all the chemo and stuff. He opted out and just let nature take her course. He's had some remissions but this time, it seems terminal.

Takes a mess of courage to go that way; a lot more dignified than throwing up all the time and losing your hair. Then, just dying anyway when you fought like hell." He shook her head.

"He looked really bad today."

"Worried sick about Greta no doubt." The Sheriff shrugged it off, but Hades could see the shadow of death on Cannon's face. Like a gray sheen that covered their faces, the soon to be dead wore it without knowing it. But, Hades could see it. He hadn't always been able to but after his days in the desert, after he had seen the living Christ, the ability had come to him.

And James Cannon had the mask of death, as he thought of it.

He went in and sat with James while they waited for death to come.

Hades spoke about God and his radiant forgiveness, his peace and all knowing acceptance. When Death came, James was ready. Hades prayed before he used the man's phone to call the Sheriff back.

The Sheriff gave him a ride back to the church. Greta had disappeared at some point, probably back to the wild. He washed his spare robe and hung it on the sagging clothesline to dry. He debated washing his shorts, but he wanted to run so he put the shorts on with a green army t-shirt. Hades put the shoes on and grabbed the pink Packers' cap.

He walked down the gravel drive to the paved road and decided he would head out of town today for his interval workout. It was a short running day but a tough workout. He came home, showered and prayed for a while.

Bored, he changed into his robe and walked into town. Coffee sounded good plus something to put in his belly. He'd gotten money from Carolyn to support his coffee habit and he tucked it into a secret compartment under his belt.

He felt a lightness in his soul. He felt sure James Cannon had received the spirit of God before he left this world. His step was light and joyous and he was at the coffee shop before he realized it.

"Hello, Friar," one of the patrons called. Only a few people were sitting at the ledge that served as a table in the coffee shop.

He ordered waffles and a coffee and spent the morning chatting with members of his flock.

News eventually filtered into the coffee shop that James Cannon had died this morning and the talk turned to his life. It reminded Hades of an informal wake. He left around noon and walked back to his cabin.

A silver Lexus was sitting in front of his cabin. Hades strode forward purposefully.

Carson Smith was hurrying from behind the church. What the hell was he doing back there?

"Got a problem Carson?" The hard edge crept into his voice. The guy absolutely was up to something and not something good.

"Ha ha, I just had to pee. Couldn't wait, sorry. I wanted to see you though. I heard you were with James Cannon when he died. Sheriff told me."

"That's accurate."

They stared at each other. Carson was taller than Hades but beefier. He had a look about him like he worked out a lot but didn't know how to use his body. It was just a thing to look at, not to use. Hades could feel the sneer pulling at his lip.

"I just wanted to make sure he went peacefully."

"Yeah, he went peacefully."

"Do you think he went to heaven?"

"I'm sure of it. You might want to examine your own readiness, Carson."

"I'm of the Hell on Earth group. I think we do our suffering here and take our joy. Then, it's just over. Blank. Black." He took a step towards Hades, clearly expecting him to back off.

Instead, Hades took a step forward and went nose to nose with him.

They stood there for a second, Hades fired up and Carson amused.

"I like you, Friar."

"Funny, I don't like you at all Smith."

Taken aback, Smith said, "I thought you had to like everyone."

"Not so. Jesus didn't like corruption when he saw it and neither do I."

Smith laughed. "You're a feisty one. I don't agree that I'm corrupt. I think that's a little harsh."

"It's easier for a camel to pass through the eye of a needle than for a rich man to get into heaven."

"Ah, that's where you're wrong: I'm not a rich man. I'm a parasite living off a rich man. My father controls all the money. What can I do? Give it all away? It's not mine."

"You're a parasite. St. Francis of Assisi was born into a rich family. He walked away from it to follow God."

"I don't believe in God. The devil? Oh, yeah. I believe in the power of evil. It's fun, in fact, to manipulate other people without their knowing it."

"How do you explain away miracles? The grand design of life? Do those things mean nothing to you?"

"I think it's all just chance. Evolution and mistakes of nature. Do you really think God has a plan for you? Was it his plan that you should become some freak show and that would help you save souls?" He laughed.

"Do you think the mischief you make stands you in good stead with your devil? Is he impressed with your petty larcenies? Wow, look he tried and failed to poison a dog. He's the man!" He mocked him broadly.

They were less than ten inches from each other. Hades saw the punch before it was thrown. The twitch of the shoulder muscle or the way Carson's eye moved alerted him. Perhaps it was just years of living on the edge of violence that made Hades turn his right shoulder toward the man attacking him and throw a vicious uppercut with his right that lifted Carson off his feet and dropped him on his pompous ass.

Even the stinging of his knuckles felt good, right somehow. It had been a long time since he'd hit anyone and damn if he hadn't missed it. He should get a heavy bag for the cabin; bleed off some frustration so he didn't knock any more of his flock on their ignorant asses.

"Hell of a way for a man of God to act." Carson spat out between gasps.

"You aren't acting like any man should act. You're acting like a spoiled little child. Get off your ass and grow up." He reached his hand down and Carson ignored it and struggled to his feet by himself.

"You're lucky I don't sue your ass!"

"Go ahead, I don't have anything but the clothes on my back. You're welcome to them." Hades whipped the robe over his back, unmindful that he was naked.

"Ugh! Put it back on, please." Carson shielded his eyes. "Jesus, you've got a lot of scars." He forgot that the man was naked in front of him and examined the scars.

Hades threw the robe back on.

"Gunshots, knife wounds and, seriously are those whip marks? Man, you're more messed up than I am." Carson laughed. "There are some real demons dancing around inside of you. Maybe you need my help, more than I need yours." He kept laughing and got in his car.

Hades looked at his fist. Instead of the righteous pain he'd felt before, his hand just hurt with stupidity.

He turned to walk back into the cabin, hesitated and then walked around the side of the church where he had seen Carson first. He saw the disturbed ground and looked down. What the hell had the creep buried? He found a stick and poked down into the soft earth. Definitely something. He dug down and found the can of rat poison. The bastard!

He wished he'd hit him harder. Demons? He'd show the jerk demons.

Carolyn came in without apparently touching the brake at all, going from 65 miles per hour to a skidding halt in front of the church. Swirling dust rose and concealed the car for a minute.

He waited until the dust settled a little before walking forward to help carry the groceries.

She jumped out of the car. "I heard James Cannon died. Mary called me. Were you with him?"

"Yes, he went peacefully and with the forgiveness of a gracious God."

"Really? He was a believer at the end? I knew him well. I just have to say I'm a little surprised by that."

"He was. I had a visit from Carson Smith. Or rather, he dug a hole on the side of the church and hid some rat poison. I saw him coming from there," he pointed. "And when he left, I went and saw the earth had been dug up and this was at the bottom of the hole."

Carolyn pursed her lips and took the can. She examined the label and handed it back to Hades. "You didn't see him bury it?"

"No, but come on! Neither one of us was here and he comes from behind the church, guilty as sin."

"He's a pillar of the community. His father basically owns the town. It wouldn't exist without that family," she muttered more to herself than to Hades.

"You don't believe me?"

"I didn't say that. I'm just saying before you make accusations, you better have proof and witnesses."

"Just be careful. That's all I'm saying."

"Are you trying to tell me to be careful in my own town?"

"Yes," he said firmly. "A man who would poison a dog would do anything."

"He just doesn't want to be here. His father shipped him here and hoped it took but it never did. He's miserable; cut him some slack. I keep hoping he'll find some nice young woman and settle down."

"He's corrupt! You don't know him like I do." Hades tried to keep his temper under control but how was it that Carolyn, an intelligent and bright woman, didn't see through him?

"So you've been here, what two weeks and you can see into everyone's soul and I've only lived here my whole life and have rosy blinders on?" She slammed the car door and left him to carry in his groceries and packages.

Should he go talk to her? Hades decided to wait until he'd cooled down a little. Otherwise, he'd just get in a fight with her again. He unloaded his groceries on the counter, put the beer and milk away and stowed the frozen dinners in the freezer. She'd bought them on her own, he hadn't asked for them but he was glad all the same. She was right: he had to eat more or his metabolism would start eating into his muscle. He had to be as strong as possible for the coming trials.

Especially if those trials included fighting Carson Smith.


"Give away my money? Ha. If Friar do gooder ever knew just how poor I am, he'd be giving me that robe." Carson kicked the chair in his apartment. His father owned everything and kept little Carson on a very short leash. He'd screwed up in New York and been shuffled out here to no man's land for his penance.

The apartment, the car, even his food was paid for out of an allowance carefully monitored by an accountant of his dad's. The reward for toeing the line and not causing problems would be a return to the bright lights of Broadway. Theoretically. His dad never set a deadline, never told him when he was finished tormenting him. Shit, the girl had been a hooker, for Christs sake!

Nobody gave a rat's butt about them and the turnover was good for everyone. Got some new talent on the street. It wasn't like his holier than thou dad didn't spring for a call-girl once in a while. But then, it was like, required for him to provide for visiting CEOs, especially the foreign ones. And not street walkers either. Dad bought the top talent, classy bitches who looked down their surgically altered noses at you but were like cats in heat for the right money.

Maybe that was Carson's mistake; not snuffing a classier piece of ass. He still didn't know how his dad had found out. He never discussed it with Carson, simply shipped him out and told him the deal. Keep your nose clean and hope things blow over. It was all tactics for dear old dad. How would it look? How would it affect business?

How would it feel to really believe in something like the Friar did? He almost envied the loser. He definitely was weirded out about all the scars on the Friar's lean body. There was something dark and naughty about the man, that was for sure.

If he was a gay, he would be in love. He should probably think about getting a girlfriend and marry. Would that fill the dark void that drove him to cruise for sluts?

The Friar said he was acting like an immature asshole and he believed that to be true even though he hated admitting it. Maybe a girlfriend would be the answer to everything that ailed him.

Were there any halfway attractive women in Fell? He didn't want a virgin, that was for sure. He didn't want anyone that had a reputation either. They had to be around his age, preferably a little younger. Marian from the church came to mind.

She was a widow maybe five years younger than him. She had a nice body, great eyes. She was a definite possibility. There was the waitress at the coffeeshop. She had two kids though. He didn't want kids or did he? If they weren't too old, it might be ok. A woman would be more interested in taking care of her kids than him and he wanted to avoid that. If he was going to go out with someone, he wanted to be the focal point of their life.

He knew that was selfish but he was honest with himself about his need to be the apex. Unlike Friar Big Dick. He had demons fighting other demons inside of his holy raiments. They just hadn't struggled to the surface yet.

Carson wondered if he should be the one to force them out. How fun that would be, to see the Friar humiliated in front of everyone. He went to bed on that pleasant note.

# Chapter Nine

By the time Hades unpacked and admired the sweatpants, Carolyn had left. He would have to thank her tomorrow before the service. He was wrong to jump on her with both feet. She wasn't used to looking at people in black and white. She was obviously a kind soul who would give a loser like Carson, the benefit of the doubt. He should have taken a softer tact with her.

It was that damned Carson's fault. He was wound up from finding the poison and his encounter with the jerk.

Hades moved his sleeping gear to the enclosed patio. It was a ten by ten room with screens covering the upper half of the walls. He hoped the the cold air would do the trick and let him sleep.

What would he do when it was winter?? Fall was one thing and it was in the thirties at night now. How cold would it get in the winter?

Well, he would try tonight and take it one day at a time. He blew out and his breath was a thin white cloud.

Whether he decided to sleep here or not, he would have to do something about the maintenance of the room. The screens were lose and he was sure the mosquitos would come in droves in the summer. The floor boards were warped and splintery.

He didn't worry about animals. Animals wouldn't attack a man, no matter what the locals liked to scare you with. He snugged up under the coverlet. He liked it already. It reminded him of the war. He had always slept well whether in the jungle or the desert. Except for those damned spiders. They still creeped him out and chased him through his dreams.

There was a moon out when he woke. It silvered the room. Hades lay still, deciding whether he needed to jump up or pretend to be asleep. There was an unaccustomed weight on his torso. Carolyn?? Oh my God!

He slid his hand down and ran it down the arm across his waist. It took a moment for his mind to make sense of the fur. He looked down and saw the twin slits of yellow eyes. Greta laid her head down again and his wiry body relaxed under her comforting weight.

He guessed Greta had made the decision to take ownership of him. Like most of the major decisions in his life, the awesome hand of God was in this. If God wanted him to have this wolf, he would fight for her.

He woke refreshed. He could do anything. Had he imagined the massive wolf last night? Like a dream wolf or something? His robe had long, sharp gray hairs over the bottom half of it. Definitely not his. Was she off hunting? Was the visitation a sign? A one-time thing and she wouldn't come back. He would have to wait and see.

The gorgeous crispness of a golden green fall day beckoned. He whipped off his robe and soaked it in the deep work sink in the garage and hung it on the broken down line. For a moment, he wasn't sure the poles would take the weight of the wet wool robe. After a wobble, the sag deepened but the poles of the drying line held. He smiled.

He was tempted to wash his other robe too but they took forever and a half to dry and he would be darned uncomfortable in a wet one. The spirit moving him to wash them happened so seldom though, he really considered it.

He did a few stretches and walked to the paved road. A blue Suburban crested the hill and turned into the lot. He saw Carolyn raise her eyebrows and look at her watch as she drove into the lot. Shit, today was Sunday. He waited till the slight cloud of dust settled around the vehicle and her door opened.

"Where are you going? It's eight thirty. Church starts in an hour and a half. You can't go off on one of those cross-country jaunts this morning."

"I'll be back in time."

"You need to have time to shower and put on a clean robe too. You can't be all, well, smelly on Sunday."

"I washed my robe but the clean one won't be dry for a few days. I'll run for twenty minutes, then shower."

"I'll take care of the robe."

"There's nothing you can do. It's wool and it's almost an inch thick. They take forever to dry. Don't worry, God won't care," he assured her. He took off a bit faster than usual. He might be sore tomorrow, but counted on fitting in some stretching before he had to speak.

He practiced his sermon as he ran, unconsciously ticking off the miles.

He turned at what he estimated was the ten-minute mark and started back. He heard the car before he saw it as it raced up the hill behind him. The back of his brain kept track of the sound, bringing it to the forefront when the noise became overwhelming. He stepped to the side of the road.

A silver Lexus flew over the hill. It seemed like it was veering towards him and he moved forward to stand behind a tree. He watched as Carson's smiling face straightened out on the road and flew away from him.

Had the asshole really aimed at him? Would he have hit him? Hades meant to have a serious talk with the jerk the next time he was him. Right now, he had a sermon to give. He picked up his pace and cleared his mind.

The church showed up on his left and he stopped running. He did some stretches off to the side, noting the presence of the silver Lexus behind him. He visualized the anger flowing out of him. The guy was annoying as hell but he didn't want to kill him. Well, ok right now, he did want to kill the guy. The danger, to his mind, was that it would be really easy to kill him. The army had given him the skills. All that held him in check was his fear of displeasing God.

Sometimes, he wondered that God was capable of loving him at all. Why would a magnificent God save him in the desert and why would that selfsame God choose him for important work. Or was God playing a small joke on him by sending him to Fell. The whole exercise completed to save James Cannon's soul and now he was a door stop until God called him home. Who was he to question God's will?

Crap, some endorphins should have kicked in by now but a blackness had descended on his soul during the run. He prayed in earnest when he walked back to his cabin to change. The robe was gone from the clothesline. Panic grabbed him.

"Friar!" Carolyn was waving to him from the church.

"Have you got my robe?"

"Yeah, I went into your home and got your other robe. I washed them both and dried them for you."

He stared at her, hands on his hips. His anger flared. How dare she? Seeing the tentative smile on her apple-doll wrinkled face, the anger seeped out of him.

"Thank you, but it's my job to wash my robes. I can't have you waiting on me."

"I'm not waiting on you. It's purely self-defense," the color rose in her cheeks, "Eau de Friar is so awful, I wanted to spare our parishioners."

"It's part of being a Friar! We are not of this world. We aren't supposed to give a shit about how we look or smell or if we eat regularly. This whole pretending to be a priest thing is wrong." He sat down on the porch, distressed.

"It's ok, Friar, we'll get through this." She sat on the step next to him and put her arm around him, then removed it. "You're all wet."

"Sweat, honest sweat. I don't fit in here." He put his head in his hands.

"Nevertheless, you are here and you're doing good here. Now, go get dressed and preach."

"Some pep talk," he smiled at her and stood up.

"Oh, let me get your robes." She went into the church and brought back a fluffy pile of brown. Tiny filaments floated up in the morning sun, buoyed by mountains of static electricity. Carson Smith followed her back out; a shit eating grin on his handsome face.

"Best not get near anything electric, padre. You might arc and hurt yourself," Carson could barely contain his laughter.

"Oh, hush," Carolyn touched his arm.

Hades took the mound, received a small shock, and looked at her. "What did you do to them?"

"Well, they were so rough, I put a little fabric softener in the wash. They're a lot softer now."

"They're not supposed to be soft," he said gently.

"Doesn't the hard wool scratch your skin?"

"It's supposed to hurt to wear it, Carolyn," Carson explained. "It's one of those gotta hurt to be holy things they do." He smirked.

"Thank you for being so considerate, Carolyn. I'd better go get ready." Cars were streaming in the parking lot. "What do you want, Carson?"

"Why to hear you preach! You've made quite an impression on me. You and I are going to be best friends." Hades was quite ready to slam his fist through the man's smiling face. It shocked the hell out of him when Carolyn slid her arm through Smith's.

"That's so nice, Carson, Hades is trying to fit in better in Fell. He can probably use your help." She smiled up at him and Hades watched the butt wipe jerk turn on the charm.

He stalked away with his fluffy robes.

Back in his cabin, he drew the top robe over his head. The wool, warm and cozy, stuck to his skin like long underwear. Had it shrunk? Crap, he would need to wash it again and pull it out on a frame. A lovely flowery fragrant rose from it when he moved. The Devil hid in fabric softener, he shook his head. The sleeves seemed tighter.

He pulled on the sleeves and they loosened a bit. He tried not to be too obvious as he pulled more vigorously. The wool was strong and could take the abuse. It was helping loosen it up.

He didn't remember much of what he said that morning. Hades remembered mostly that a spark from the static of his robe had shorted out the public address system. He had heard a snorting giggle which he suspected came from Carson Smith. He solved the problem by walking up and down the center aisle of the church talking more than preaching.

He remembered that somewhere around quarter to noon, men got up and started leaving; not one or two but many. It was well after his sermon and the two readings, so they were scooting out on the closing hymns and benediction.

Petri Thomas explained it to him when he arrived a little after noon, to find the game already in progress.

"They're going to watch the kick-off. You're lucky they came to church at all. Their wives probably made them come to church. You're still a novelty. When that wears off, you'll have trouble filling a dozen pews on game day."

"Why not make church start at 10:30? Over by 11:30 back home by kickoff?"

"Father wasn't a football fan. Wouldn't have none of it. You might be better off, if you're in a changing mood, to make it start at 10. That way they can get some tailgating in before the game."

"Ten it is. Would that factor in your decision to come to church favorably?"

Petri cackled at him. He tried his first-ever brat covered in sauerkraut and pronounced it superb. Against his better judgment, he tried cheese curds.

"The jury is still out on the curds but the brats are amazing."

"You'll want to take some Pepto home with you for later," she warned him.

"Will the brats be revisiting me tonight?"

"They tend to stay with you," she told him ominously.

At halftime, the Packers were ahead and Petri turned to him.

"Quiz time. Who's in our division?"

"Bears, Vikings, Lions," he told her.

"QB?" She ran him through the basics, was pleased and asked him to get another beer for them both.

He hadn't been interested in sports for a long time and he found the changes to the sport fascinating; even the rules had changed.

"Back when I played, if you got laid out, you were expected to go back in the next play after you regained consciousness."

"Those were the good old days when ignorance was bliss. Now, they found out all those old players are dying from depression and mental issues." She shook her head. "They'll probably ban football one of these days. "I hope to be cold in the ground before then."

The Packers won and Petri told him he should thank God for it.

"Spousal abuse goes up dramatically with a Packer loss. Crime does too."

"I'll add it to my prayers. Do you need anything before I head out?"

"Head out? There's another game, woosie!"

How she was still functioning with all the beer she'd drunk. He'd had six and she had matched and more what he'd drunk. He was six two and 180 pounds and she ran about five foot five, he guessed and 160 pounds. She appeared unimpaired.

They had more brats for dinner chased down with beer. He had them naked without the sauerkraut and hoped for the best. He wished he hadn't driven so he could run home, run some of the grease and alcohol out of his system. In fact, he stopped drinking when it occurred to him that he'd driven there. He considered leaving the Bronco there and running anyway. He couldn't get behind the wheel like this. His two choices were stay the night or walk home. Embarrassment burned in his face and he shook his head. What a mess he'd made of it.

His focus blurred and the second game was hazy to him. Her voice floated past him. She spoke in a monotone which made it harder to concentrate on her words. Petri commented on every play. It didn't seem like she even expected him to respond. He closed his eyes for a moment. It's been a long time since he'd drunk that much beer.

The light of dawn peeking over the ridge and into Petri's front room woke him. He sat upright on the couch and someone, he presumed Petri had thrown a crocheted afghan over him. His bladder was at capacity as if it was going to explode and he threw off the cover and lurched to the bathroom. His head pounded and his mouth was dry and tasted like old dust.

He peed for three minutes straight and judged that he might live if his head would stop spinning. He washed his hand and his face. The ruined side tingled and burned a little when the cool water hit it. He opened the door and the aroma of coffee drew him to the kitchen.

"You look a might peaked today, Hades. Coffee?" He followed the voice to the tiny kitchen. A small round table looked out over a backyard of pines and scrub bushes.

"Man, I can't drink like that anymore. I'm too old." He sat and accepted the aspirin and coffee. He wondered if he should deny himself the aspirin as a measure of his sin.

"Take it. No need to suffer needlessly."

"As a Friar, I'm responsible for my own sin. I can't just wash it away with aspirin. That's too easy. Friars are all about suffering."

"Well, seeing as we've spent the night together, may I offer some advice?"

"Spent the night?" His jaw dropped open.

"Yeah, in a manner of speaking. Plus, I'm old and I have a perspective on things you don't yet, Friar or not"

Hades gestured for her to go ahead. To argue would be too painful.

"You'll find there's plenty of suffering in the world to go around. Take your ease where you can, when you can. Tough times are ahead and no mistake."

A light mist had started falling when Hades hit the turnoff and had to make the choice to either go into town or back to the cabin.

He decided he would drop by the coffee shop and catch up on the local news. He parked at the end of the block. Every other space was occupied. His robe was soaked by the time he got there. Actually a good thing, he could hang it in his bathroom and allow it to stretch out again.

Standing room only, not a good sign in a small town. When people realized he was in the room, they began to move away from him. Evidently, the fabric softener new as summer rain was wearing off.

"Padre, I was just telling everyone that another girl is missing. This one from Fell. Makayla worked at the diner. She's 16 and she lives in Auburn Manor trailer park. Mom hasn't seen her since yesterday. She was working as a dishwasher at the diner after school every day. Usually walks home after working a few hours, it's usually still light when she sets out.

"She's a straight A student, one of the good ones, although it wouldn't matter if she was a juvenile offender. If anyone knows anything or if anyone has seen her, I want to hear about it."

Hades noticed when the first girl turned out to be from the next town over, they had dismissed the danger from their collective brain. This abduction felt different. The first had the giddy excitement of a dangerous ride. This one had the sinking horror of a personal nightmare.

"I think I saw her walking home Friday night. I went back and was going to offer her a ride."

"Why didn't you? Just curious." The Sheriff watched his face closely.

"Because she was a young girl. I didn't want anyone to misconstrue me picking her up. As a Friar, I'm held to a higher standard. Man, I have to be careful, but by the time I got home, I regretted it. Jesus would have said, to hell with it and picked her up. So I went back but she wasn't on the road anymore."

There was some murmuring and Hades wondered if he should have said anything. He certainly wasn't doing himself any favors with these people.

People started drifting into small groups, talking by twos and threes, giving sidelong looks at Hades. He looked right back at them, hoping his light was shining through. The brats and sauerkraut were still sitting in a big greasy ball right at the bottom of his stomach.

Coffee lost its appeal, but he nodded his thanks for the cup the owner pushed at him. It was warm at least and the chill from the wet robe was pressing on him. He sipped a little to make room and added as much cream as the cup would take.

"I didn't do anything to that girl, Sheriff." The Sheriff pulled up a chair to sit with him.

"I'm of half a mind to believe you, son. Under that man of God robe, I think you've seen some rough things. I just can't see you hurting a little bitty girl somehow."

"Thank God!"

"I got to be honest with you though. You coming to our town coincided with the other girl showed up in the quarry and James' dog getting poisoned. Well, people think even if you weren't involved with the bad things somehow you're connected to them. But, as far as I'm concerned, I need some help and you seem like you might have acquired exactly the skills I need."

"What do you mean?"

"I need someone who can go behind the scenes unofficially like and investigate where I can't. You were a scout. Isn't that something you'd be pretty good at?"

Hades closed his eyes in distress. He was absolutely sure Father Xavier didn't have this in mind when he sent him to Fell. Miss Carolyn's disproving image appeared in his mind and he sucked in his breath. "It's not really what I do now."

"Listen up. We're in this together whether you realize it or not. This town is ready to ride you out of town on a rail if they even so much as think it might help bring that girl home. She wasn't some throw away prostitute that half the people privately see as having it coming. She was our future, our bright promise of eternity and you and I need to find her."

"Only I'm not exactly equipped. I wasn't even alive the last time this town had a murder. The state guys already ripped me a new one for moving the quarry girl without doing everything by the book. I don't even have a God damned book. I got this job because I have emphysema and can't work in the quarry. So, let's work on this together, ok? You help me out and I'll do my best to put a good word in for you with Miss Carolyn and the rest of the town. What do you say?"

"I'll do whatever I can to help you. Tomorrow, bring everything you have down to the cabin. Any of the paperwork and test results available. Today, let's get some volunteers out to look. The weather is crappy, but on the chance she's still in the area, we need to do something. We'll need maps so we can come up with a plan."

"Thank you, son. We'll find that girl." People started moving when Hades barked out orders. Someone ran for a map and he gathered some markers.

He spread out the topographic map on the counter.

"I'm not familiar with this area except where I've run. Where would be a place he could have privacy? A guy goes to all the trouble to snatch some woman, he isn't going to throw away the chance to play a little bit. He isn't going to kill her right away, if it's the same guy who did the quarry girl. He's going to want to hurt her first. A lot."

The Sheriff grimaced and took a step toward Hades. "You're a little scary son. How fast you got into his head."

Several of the men who had volunteered to spend some time in the wet woods looking for the girl showed shock on their faces that the Friar would talk that way.

But he could see most of them thinking about places they knew.

"Go there. The first place that popped into your head. Look for sign. Most of you have hunted?" When they nodded, he nodded too. "Don't go in. This guy is a predator. He may have laid traps, booby traps for anyone coming around. I know I would."

"What do we do then?"

"Use your cell phone. Call it in to the Sheriff. Call whether you saw anything or not so we know you aren't hanging on a meat hook somewhere."

He said it to show them how serious it was. This wasn't some fun hunt in the woods where you saw how much beer you could drink.

"Everyone needs to write down where you're going to check. The Sheriff will have the list and then we'll come find you if you don't check in within an hour. Is that enough time?" Nods all around.

Back in his cabin, he took off the wet robe and hung it on the bar in the bathroom. He put on the other robe and went outside for a few minutes until it had a fine mist standing up on it. He pulled on it to stretch it out again.

Hades knew he was under watch. It made sense that the Sheriff would want to keep him close if he were under suspicion. The Sheriff probably thought that Hades might let something slip. He arranged for Hades to go with him.

"This does all seem to be connected to me," he said to the Sheriff once they were in his Suburban.

"I think so too."

"It swirls around like some kind of sick greasy mess but I don't quite see the beginning of it. It had to start with some kind of anger before I ever got here. That girl who was beat up and left in the quarry. This guy didn't even know me then."

They were headed out to a fishing spot that the Sheriff knew. It was very private, very secluded and he thought it showed promise of hiding someone since he felt few people would go there at this time of the year.

"Then, it seems like it refocused itself on me as an easy target. Damn! Let's turn around." Hades was looking around for an easy place for the vehicle to turn around.

"You got something to say, say it."

"I don't want to accuse anyone prematurely. But I think we ought to look around my cabin and the church. Are there any good places around there?"

"Son, there are places all over these hills. We could go up behind your cabin, if you're up for a hike."

"I think we'd better."

"If we find her there, it's going to be mighty hard for you to explain."

"Or easy to explain. Someone is trying to frame me, not because they hate me but because I'm convenient. And I know who it is. If we find her there alive, she'll tell you who grabbed her."

"And if she's dead?" The Sheriff asked.

"I'll take care of it myself."

"How long you been a man of the cloth? Pardon me if I ask but you got a mouth on you."

"Ordained? Not long. I spent a few years going through all the steps and then took my vows. I wanted to stay in New York City. I thought I fit in pretty well with the poor there, but Father Xavier assigned me here, so here I am."

"Like forever?"

"You mean, are you stuck with me?" Hades laughed. "Until they reassign me or, alternatively, just leave me here forever."

"Has Miss Carolyn been making a lot of trouble for you?" The Sheriff smiled as they turned into the church lot and parked at the cabin.

"Let's just say, I feel her critical eye on me. But, I can only be what I am and do the best I can for God."

"Do you need to change? The terrain is pretty rough up there." He pointed behind the cabin at the wall of trees going up onto the moraine.

"I put on some boots. Want a beer?"

The Sheriff thought about it for a moment. "Best not. Maybe afterward."

The Sheriff led the way up a narrow dirt trail behind Hades' cabin. He took out his inhaler after about twenty steps. "Emphysema."

Hades' cardio was awesome from running and he wondered how long this search was going to take with the Sheriff.

"Do you want me to go ahead?"

"No offense, but that wouldn't do much good, would it? If you're the perp," he gasped.

"No offense," shot back Hades, "but with your emphysema, this is going to take all day. And that's just if you don't end up in the emergency room. We need to check in within the hour."

"Shit," he breathed out. "Go ahead. I'll stay right here."

"I'm going to start at the top and work my way down", Hades explained. Then, he strode past him easily, eating up the hill. He was at the top in less than a minute.

The wind played on the hair growing in on his head. It felt cool on the scarred side of his face. He wouldn't mind just running away. Miss Carolyn hated his guts because he wasn't a priest, the Sheriff suspected him of ruining the town just because some sick fuck had targeted him for hate and then there was the sick fuck himself. Why did he pick Hades to hate? It just didn't make any sense. He didn't hate Hades, he couldn't. He didn't even know Hades.

So what would be the point? Hades made his way carefully down as he thought. What was the point of targeting a Friar the man didn't even know? It was just hate for hate's sake. All it did was hurt the town.

He smiled, maybe that was the point. Who hated the town? He walked carefully, making hardly a noise at all. He still had skills and could move soundlessly.

Hades saw a disturbance in the leaves ahead and knew it was man made. He knelt in the dried leaves and listened but heard nothing.

He could call the Sheriff up or he could say there was nothing and come back later. Decisions, decisions. He was great at subterfuge physically like sneaking around, but lying went against his convictions.

"Sheriff, I see a trap here about one third down from the top." Hades stood up and waved his position down to the Sheriff. He brushed away the dead leaves to expose the edge of a pit. Otherwise, he was afraid the Sheriff would suspect him of planting the trap. Hades' level of expertise in tracking was legendary in the secretive military units with which he worked.

It was a solid ten minutes before the Sheriff came up.

"You didn't do this, did you?" Sheriff said after catching his breath.

"If I did, I wouldn't show it to you," countered Hades. "There were some leaves over it. Let's see what kind of trap we have." He took a stick and probed the area beyond the edge of the trap. Some tan canvas gave way to a hole approximately three feet by three and six feet deep. "They call this a tiger pit." He pulled the rest of the canvas away and they both stared at the body of the girl at the bottom. She was curled up in the fetal position, her naked limbs covered with dirt.

"Christ, I was hoping we'd find her alive." The Sheriff shook his head.

"I'll go down."

"Naw, you'd be disturbing the scene. Those assholes yelled at me for fouling the scene. We'll take pictures and then call them."

Her eyes fluttered open and both men sprung into action. Hades slid carefully over the side of the hole, showering more dirt on the woman. He heard the Sheriff calling for an ambulance.

"Hey, there, you're going to be all right." Hades knelt to the side in the sliding dirt. He heard her whimper and her eyes closed. Hades took her hand in his and she didn't withdraw it.

The hole reminded him of dozens of others he had dug and taken shelter in across jungles and deserts. The holes didn't change that much and he could feel a wave of cold anger growing in him that someone had stuck this girl in this hole to die.

She had been beaten badly, that much he could see just by looking at her. Here and there across her pale skin a vicious welt ran, angry and red with a clear fluid running from some of them. She had been beaten with fists and whipped. The anger boiled and then cooled again. He narrowed his eyes and was glad that the girl had her eyes closed.

"Who did this to you?" Hades bent and whispered. He thought he knew but needed confirmation to act.

She looked up at him in confusion, bright blue eye vivid in her pale dirty face. "I don't know, he wore a mask." She closed her eyes against memory and began to cry. Hades had seen and done some awful things but none of them cut into his already lacerated soul more than hurting an innocent.

Hades wanted to help her but he was concerned she had broken bones and he might make it worse. So he sat and waited.

The sun moved across the deep hole before the ambulance crew made it up the hill behind Hades' cabin. The Sheriff had sent down his jacket and Hades laid it over the girl.

Hades talked quietly to the girl while they waited. He couldn't know if she heard him but he talked anyway. He talked about his childhood and high school to when he entered the army. He skipped over the really bad parts and jumped to when he met Jesus in the desert. He talked about coming to Fell and how it hadn't been his idea of a picnic, but God had other plans, apparently.

"OK, father since you're already down there, we'll have you check her for broken bones and bleeding. Run your hands up her arm and see if you feel any broken bones for me."

Hades did as he was bid. He did the arms, legs and then sat the girl up in the hole. Her eyes opened as if she was surprised he was still there.

"Honey, does your neck hurt at all? How about your back?"

The girl shook her head no to each question.

"Let's get you up out of there. Father can you hand her up to us." A woman in her late 30s or early 40s in a dark blue uniform spoke. He saw there were two attendants, the other an older man, dressed the same.

"If I bend my knee, can you use it like a step? Then I'll cup my hands and boost you up." When she nodded he went to one knee in the cramped space. She was shaky but she put her hand on his head to steady herself and then put her other foot in the stirrup he created. She weighed next to nothing and Hades lifted her out of the hole by bringing his hands up to his face level.

The two paramedics took her from there and gave her a warm blanket before carrying her down the side of the hill. Hades boosted himself out of the hole, grabbing the Sheriff's hand for help.

The two men stood watching the paramedics carry the small girl in the blue blanket down the game trail. Her dirty blond hair trailed down the back of the blanket.

"I'm going up top. I had a thought that this creep might have staked out a surveillance spot. He rigged a trap for someone or something."

"I'll go with you. You'll have to help me over some of the rough spots."

"Not a problem. You could wait here and I could tell you if I find anything; save you the air," Hades offered.

"I've got a real sick feeling we're going to find a place where he sat watching that hole. Maybe waiting for some animal to fall in and find his next meal. There are a ton of coyote and even the odd wolf around here, not to mention things with teeth and claws that would tear a young girl with soft skin in their terror to get out."

"Come on, let's go. I had some other thoughts while I was down there."

"You mean, other than you are gonna rip his head off when you find him?"

Hades grinned at the Sheriff. " I think the first girl was just an impulsive kill. He had the opportunity and it was too good to pass up. He dumped her in the quarry because it represents everything he hates about this town. He hates this town very badly. When we find out who really despises Fell, we'll find our asshole."

"Then, someone tried to poison Greta, James Cannon's dog. Now, the man was dying and sooner rather than later. Why take the one thing he loves? Because you hate this town and everyone in it, that's why. Greta came by the church to sleep the night before last, by the way."

"Damn. It'd be better if she just kept going. He always maintained she was a dog that looked like a wolf but I've seen plenty of wolves and that dog is a wolf. Well, you know what I mean."

"Now, this girl is the first direct attack trying to link to me. He doesn't like me being here either. Nothing personal, you understand, but I represent something. Miss Carolyn getting her way and making this town something special by having the pull to get an actual priest. He hates anything that puts this town in a good light."

The Sheriff followed up after Hades, taking frequent rests to breathe. "You might be right. I'm not saying you are but I'm not saying you aren't either. I know you didn't kill the first one and I'd bet my rifle you didn't dig this hole and put this girl in. I was watching your face when you saw her down there. Even with that melted side that doesn't show much, I knew you'd kill whoever did this to that little girl, yup," he nodded.

"Some people just need killing."

"No argument here." They reached the crest and Hades started looking around. He located the position of the hole below them and moved diagonally until he found some sign and called the Sheriff over

"Someone squatted here. See the depth of the toes of the shoes? All their weight was on them."

"Seems a little dense if he wanted an animal to find his trap. "

"I think he was just checking once in a while to see if the canvass cover was gone. This guy is no hunter. No way. He didn't choose the most well travelled game trail when he set it up; it looks to me like he picked the softest ground, easiest to dig."

"I believe you're right, son."

"So, we're looking for someone who hates this town. Has hated it for a good long time and doesn't hunt."

"Narrows it down a bit in Fell."

Miss Carolyn was waiting for them under a black umbrella when they made their way down the moraine. Her lips were pursed in displeasure, her white hair was pulled back severely, although a few stray wisps had escaped and curled up in the humidity. It softened her somehow. It was a measure of her distraction that her reading glasses perched on her nose. Too vain to wear them most of the time, thought Hades.

Going down was a lot easier for the Sheriff; he only had to stop a few times. Hades waited with him each time as if he had to stop too. He knew it wasn't fooling Miss Carolyn but if it gave the Sheriff a little face, that was enough for Hades.

"That was that girl, wasn't it?" She barely waited until they were in earshot.

"Yup, it was her," answered the Sheriff. "Someone beat her up and put her in a six-foot deep hole. Looks like they were hoping some wild animal would get in there with her and finish her off. Didn't have the stones for murder." Sheriff shook his head.

"Did you do it, Friar?" She tried to look down her nose at him, but he towered over her.

"No, but someone is trying to make it look like I did."

"And exactly how are we supposed to know that you didn't do it?"

"Because if I was going to do it, you would never have found her."

Looking like she had a sour taste in her mouth, Miss Carolyn turned on her heel and went back to the church.

# Chapter Ten

He hated waiting. There wasn't anyone to share his plan with and it was hard to hide his excitement. He had seen that stupid wolf coming down from the mountain the other day. And it had actually looked into the cabin window. It was too much to hope that it was looking for the Friar to eat him. It probably liked the Friar's aroma, much like dirt and garbage.

That gave him the idea with the girl. He wouldn't even have to kill her. It was a long shot but he imagined the wolf would be curious about the hole with meat in it. He had angled the sides of the lip inward.

In his dream, the wolf would fall in, become desperate and eat the girl. Was it so impossible? It wasn't out of the realm of possibilities, was it? Well if the wolf didn't find her, no one would until the odd boy scout stumbled upon the hole, breaking his tiny little leg. He hoped the town had folded in on itself by then and been repurposed into a boy scout camp.

It wouldn't happen while there was still a quarry producing valuable gravel, though. He pondered how he could stop it. He understood more about the quarry than people gave him credit for. People underestimated him all the time.

How to ruin the mine? He took out some wine and let it breathe. The quarry had operated for over a hundred years. It was the source of his family's wealth and his continued ability to do absolutely nothing for the rest of his life.

It was a dilemma. He walked around the beautiful Tudor style house that had been built by someone a long time ago in his family who was vastly more talented than him. He appreciated it, really.

Carson considered becoming an integral part of the quarry. Really dig in and work on managing it and then, when his father had the inevitable coronary in his fifties like all the Smith men, he would let everyone go and sell the quarry.

If he sold it with the stipulation that they not hire any local people... No, that would never work. The new owners couldn't be expected to bus in workers. He touched the wine, not quite warm enough.

Would Miss Carolyn help him? She held a lot of sway in this rinky dink town. Her great great whatever had founded the damned town with Carson's great great whatever. They had dug the first rock and staked their claims.

He poured some wine, swung it around the glass and considered the problem.

Miss Carolyn hated everyone. In this they were kindred souls. What if he confided in her? Probably not. She might balk at the kidnapping of the girl. Definitely would balk at the wolf eating girl.

Rumor had it she was trying to get the Friar recalled. She had expected a priest and they sent a Friar. In some subtle way, she had failed the town, Miss high and Mighty Carolyn. She practically expected people to genuflect. Whereas people treated him like shit. Somehow, the way his father felt about him transferred to how the quarry workers treated him and that was most of the town acting like he was a red-headed stepchild that nobody would speak of.

The fuckers. He would make them all pay, if he could. The Friar was throwing a wrench into things. Getting rid of the Friar was first, but what was next? It was hard to figure out how to pull the underpinnings out from under the town without hurting himself momentarily. Selling the mine would be awesome if his father would just die.

# Chapter Eleven

The big beast walked down the hill on her rough, padded feet. A casual observer wouldn't have heard her if she'd passed without five feet of him. There was the hole. She nosed it, knowing that someone new had been there: the man. She breathed a little faster and her tail wagged a couple of times. He smelled of musk and man and sweat, a unique scent that only he had. The man was strong; she could respect the man. He really knew how to scratch behind the ears.

She pawed a little here and there; others had been here but she wasn't interested in them. The scent she was looking for was there but buried. She needed to refresh the hate scent.

The Longtime Man died the same day the bad meat came. The smell associated with the bad meat belonged to evil and she was determined to find him and take a chunk out of whoever was on the other end of that smell. She associated that smell with the death of the Longtime Man and it made a growl rumble up through her big chest.

The Strong Man sometimes slept in the screened-in porch below. The Longtime Man had never let her sleep with him. She would wander down and check later if he was there. His scent came up to her from below and the wolf drank it in. Her tail wagged twice and she continued her survey of the ground until she found the Hate scent isolated. She drank it in, storing it so she could recognize it. She knew it usually took two separate scentings before something became imprinted.

Suddenly, she wanted to see the Strong Man. She trotted down and followed his trail to the cabin. She was tall enough to stand and look in the windows, but she didn't see him. There! A mouse ran across the floor. A growl stopped it in its tracks. She could see the tiny nose twitching and wondered if she could break the window and kill it. Would it please Strong man?

It disappeared into the wall and she forgot it. The Strong Man's scent went to the parking lot and she circled a couple of times. Where had he gone? She wandered off to catch something to eat. Hunting was a full time job without the Longtime Man to hunt for her. She wondered if the Strong Man would provide food for her, if she found him. She smelled something, nose high she followed the delicious scent of squirrel up the hill again.

# Chapter Twelve

He tried to stop himself from driving over to Smith's and beating the living shit out of him but found himself in the Bronco anyway. But, really, he argued with himself, wasn't that just what that butt hole wanted? Be reasonable, he thought, he didn't even know where the man lived.

He pulled into the parking lot at the coffee shop. May as well get up to date on the day's latest doings.

He walked in and heads turned, checking out the new entry. The owner brought a coffee for him. Hades soaked in the ambience, grateful for the moment that no one came and sat with him.

He needed a moment to refocus himself on God. His God would guide him through this. He counted them off on his hands, inconspicuously. Miss Carolyn hated him because he wasn't a priest and she felt it reflected badly on her prestige. Carson Smith hated him because he was bored and it was fun. The Sheriff hated him not because he really thought he was responsible for the two girls being hurt but because his arrival had upset the balance of the town and set a psycho off on a path of destruction. On the plus side, James Cannon had gone to God. He thought he had a decent chance of helping the Fellows sisters and Petri Thomas.

Really, he thought, if people got past his ruined face, he was not so bad a person. Correction, he was really a horrible albeit repentant person who had come to God late but had come finally. He meant to drag as many to God as possible to make up for those he had killed for the sake of his country.

Or at least, that's the line they had fed him as a green recruit so many moons ago. And he had followed them like theirs was the only truth in the whole wide world.

"More coffee, sugar?"

"I'm anything but sweet, Marcy," Hades held out his cup for a refill.

"What's going on in your little world, pastor? You seem 93 million miles away. That's the distance from the Earth to the sun."

"I had no idea," the laugh burbled out of Hades.

"Online learning. I love astronomy. I'm a real fan." She topped off cups in the immediate area without asking if anyone wanted more. The fluidity and economy of movement was graceful.

"That's amazing. I like looking at the stars, but they are just pretty twinkling points in the sky to me. I don't know anything about them. Did you hear the Sheriff and I pulled that girl out of a hill behind my cabin?" May as well get it over with, he thought.

"Yeah, we're tuned into the emergency radio band in back. Didn't say they found her in a hole though." Marcy set the coffee down and pulled out a seat.

"Yeah, creep put her in a hole on a game trail and then put a cloth over it probably hoping some animal would fall in and finish her off. He's one sick pig. He hates this town something fierce, that I know."

"Yeah, that speaks of a powerful hate."

"And not a lot of hunting experience. Sound like anyone in town?"

"No, but I'll think about it. Most people around here can hunt, gut a kill and eat a hearty lunch while doing it. A real hunter would have known an animal wouldn't fall into that lame-ass trap." Marcy picked up the coffee pot and made sure all the cups were filled, but he knew her heart wasn't in it. He could tell she was thinking about it. Word would get around, he knew. Marcy was not the type to keep silent, especially with gossip from the new 'pastor.'

He smiled. They could call him whatever the hell they wanted as long as they came to God. If they wouldn't come to church, he would touch them wherever they hung out or with home visits. He felt immeasurably better about his mission having spread some traps about for Carson. Soon, others would start thinking about him as a suspect.

It would be better if the thought didn't come from him, but arose naturally amongst his own people. Hades smiled with the half of his face that was still mobile. God is good.

He saw Marcy leaning her hip on the table talking to two men in flannel and hunting caps. He sipped the coffee slowly. He might have to stay here the whole day to properly get the idea moving. Fuck Carson if he thought he could hurt people in this town and just sit back and enjoy the show.

Hades had seen guys like Carson in the armed services. They often ended up on point like Hades did but for different reasons. Hades just didn't trust anyone else with his life, knowing himself to be more alert, more careful and just more attuned than others. Other guys he had seen 'nominated' to be point man were nominated because they were obnoxious, pains in the ass and needed to be dead soon as nominated by their fellow soldiers.

His platoon was happy to have him lead; their survival rate was better. So far, his little town wasn't doing so well but he had the honor to be their point man and he would see their survival rate improve. No matter what he had to do.

Miss Carolyn pushed open the door to the coffee shop. All heads turned but she didn't acknowledge any of them. She saw the Friar, got her coffee and stood by his table.

With a sigh, Hades stood and said, "Would you like to sit with me, Miss Carolyn?"

She set her white cup down and sat down in the chair.

She'd already made it plain she cared nothing about his personal life. Only his public personna mattered and only in that it reflected upon her. "So, what's new?"

"Did our lame-brained Sheriff come up with that or did you have to help him out?"

"Does it matter? It's the truth as we know it so far. Who do you know who hates the town enough to risk murder?"

"Just about anyone who got tired of hard work and ran away."

"So, help me out here. I don't belong here, as you've often pointed out. Who fits the bill?"

She considered the steam rising from her coffee. "I don't want to point the finger at anyone." She said, quietly. Her lips pursed and she looked troubled.

"Come on, Carolyn. He put a sixteen year old girl in a hole, hoping a wild animal would fall in and savage her. The other girl, the one dumped in the quarry didn't make it. Who's going to be next? Do you want that on your conscience?" Hades' voice raised and he realized everyone was looking at him.

"I'll think about it." Carolyn said quietly. Hades picked up his cup and brought it to the counter.

"Good day, Carolyn." He knew it would hurt her to have to sit alone. He wanted her to think about what might happen in the town, if she took Carson's side in this mess. She was the key to shining a light on Carson's role just like she was a barometer of the town's pulse. Let her stew of her position for a while. He prayed she would come to the right decision.

He could easily and competently take out Carson without anyone knowing. It was still on the table as an option but not the most preferred option. It would be best if the townspeople came to the realization of his guilt on their own.

If he tipped his hand, people here might never trust him. He had to look at the bigger picture. He wouldn't allow another attack, whether he had to step in or not.

He stopped at the door and turned back to look at Miss Carolyn. Although she didn't look at him directly, he knew her eyes were on him. He felt petty standing there trying to punish an older woman. He picked up his coffee cup and went back to the table.

"You seem a mite conflicted, Friar. I don't care for a man who can't make up his mind. Shows a certain lack of character, if you ask me." She smiled smugly.

He smiled too. She was a wily old bitch who had everyone wrapped around her finger. He would give her this round.

The Sheriff came in and came right over to Miss Carolyn's table. "Ma'am, Friar, just wanted to let you know that the girl doesn't remember anything. Doc says it isn't unusual in a severe beating. She may or may not ever remember who did this to her."

"Was there any skin under her nails?"

The Sheriff's face tightened up. He got up and shook his head. "You got any other great ideas?"

"Did they check for fibers on her, in the hole? Hades hated himself for making the suggestion but the Sheriff just didn't have the expertise to solve this case. He amended his thought: he'd already solved it he just needed to point everyone else in the right direction and make them think it was their idea.

"Afternoon, ma'am, Friar, looks like I've got my work cut out for me. Let me know if you get any other brain farts, Hades." He pushed back and took a sip from his coffee.

"I need to get back home too," Miss Carolyn stood up and adjusted a pale scarf around her neck.

Hades thought he may as well get a run in today. He drove up and got out. His spidey sense was tingling. Something was wrong but he couldn't put a name to it. It was too quiet. Even the birds were silent. He bent to fix his sandal.

Nothing was wrong with it but it gave him shelter on his six while he scanned the area before him. He heard a cough, like someone with a boatload of phlegm in their throat...

He spun, still kneeling and came eye to eye with Greta. She stuck her nose under his chin and pushed. Hades scrubbed the back of her ears and she leaned her not inconsiderable weight into him. He heard her sigh, felt the coarse hair on her sides move in and out.

He bent his head down and pushed back on her. Greta jumped back and leaned back on her strong back haunches. Hades jumped at her with his arms spread wide and threatening. She danced back and then lunged in snapping. He grabbed her one ear as she went past and rubbed the side of her head. He almost fell as she leaned towards him. He smiled and Greta licked the bad side of his face, gently like she wasn't sure it was allowed.

Greta talked to him then; at least that's how he interpreted it. She nuzzled him and talked. If he could only speak wolf! He imagined she was telling him that James Cannon was gone and she missed him. He missed the man too.

He wondered if Greta intended to stay with him. If so, he'd have to think of providing meat for her. He could look up how much she was supposed to eat every day, he supposed.

Did he want a pet? Did it violate any of his vows? He didn't think so but he couldn't be sure. Poverty, Chastity and Obedience. Greta probably wouldn't want to live in the house anyway. He hoped people wouldn't shoot at her, but he wasn't betting against it. He would have to ask how James Cannon kept her with these trigger happy folks hunting everywhere.

In the meantime, he would pray and take dinner. He fixed a chop and cut it in half. Greta lounged on the porch and he pulled up his sermon table.

Hades ate first and then offered the wolf the other half. She took it eagerly. Her hunting was probably rusty after being with Cannon all these years.

Tomorrow, he would bring it up with Miss Carolyn. She knew everything about her town. After dinner, he might work on his sermon a bit and then retire. He had always liked the idea of rising with the sun and sleeping when it got dark, making the smallest carbon footprint he could manage.

He slept on the covered porch and watched Greta do a close perimeter walk and then do one large circle on a bigger perimeter. She was a good partner and he hoped Miss Carolyn approved. How could she not, and what was the alternative? Putting her down was not an option.

He slept in fits and starts, his subconscious worrying about the wolf. In his dreams, people shot at them, poisoned them, set vicious traps for them and skinned them. He woke with Greta's yellow eyes on him. She laid down next to him and one side of his body heated instantly.

She smelled of woods and musk and freedom and for a moment, he wished he could just run away. Then, he went back to a deep sleep.

# Chapter Thirteen

"So, how is the guy?" Her brother's nasally voice came through the line. How he had adopted that hideous New York accent was beyond her. Really, he had been brought up better than that, she thought. They spoke on the phone every week at this time. Much more than he spoke to the silly fluff that was his wife.

"He had the most horrible hair cut I've ever seen. I took him straight to the barber in the airport. He ran a shaver over his head but he missed some spots. He'd be fairly handsome if he let his hair grow in."

"Sounds like you've taken him under your wing," he said.

"He smells. He wears the same rough brown robe every day. And he runs."

"In the robe?"

"No, silly, he wears those tiny running shorts that men do and a T-shirt. He's really fast and he runs for hours. It's impressive, even as it is abhorrent."

"Sounds pretty normal to me. I can look out my window and see guys running like that, their faces all in pain like. Never appealed to me."

"Half his face was burned by Iraqi torturers."

"What?"

"Really, it's like half his face is a reddish mass of running skin. It scares people. And then there's this eye staring out at you. Creepy. He told the story in his first sermon. Said he knew everyone was wondering so he talked about how they'd held him for days and dripped acid on his face."

"Damn. I wish I could see this guy. Can he preach?"

Carolyn considered. "He really isn't bad at preaching. He more talks to the congregation. He doesn't talk down to anyone. People seem to take to him. He was a veteran and that scores very high with a lot of people around here."

"Sounds like he's ok. Father Xavier called the other day. He might have someone else for you, a real priest. You'll have to keep an eye on him though."

"Great. What's wrong with him?"

"They don't come out and tell you but it sounds like some porn on the computer and maybe a little drug use. He looks like everybody's idea of a priest though. He's tall and dignified, except when he's stoned or surfing kiddie porn."

Carolyn considered. She liked a priest who looked like a priest. "Porn? Is he going to abuse little children here?"

"Nah, everybody downloads porn."

"I don't," Carolyn said archly. At least the Friar wasn't a problem that way. He smelled and was unsightly, but she felt in her heart he was earnest and dedicated to God.

"I think we'll keep our Friar a little bit longer."

"Well, don't wait too long if you want this other guy. He's not on the market yet but a real priest? Someone is going to snap him up, kiddie porn and all."

Carolyn leaned back and thought about her choices. What was best for her and the town, in that order?

Crunching, he thought, someone is crunching something tasty. The noise had woken him and his stomach rumbled. He cracked one eye and saw Greta's enormous back hunched over something. His stomach did a quick roll as he realized it must be a mouse or some other rodent and he sat up.

Sliding off the hard bench, he knelt in prayer. God would give him strength to deal with this town and especially with Miss Carolyn. He had decided to work on her again today, see if anything he had said last night at the coffee shop made an impression on her.

Greta spared him a guilty look and dropped the remains of the mouse at his feet. Hades patted her head and left the patio. He wasn't in the mood for fresh mouse. He'd eaten worse though in bleak, frightening places where he ate to survive and to provide fuel for another hour of that survival.

There was a frost on the grass and it crunched under his sandals. He would have to get a couple of blankets for when it got really cold. In contrast, the heat of his cabin buffeted him as he opened the door. How low could you turn the thermostat without freezing the pipes? He rolled it down to sixty-two and made a mental note to ask at the coffee house this morning.

He opened the fridge, realizing he really hadn't eaten since breakfast yesterday. Miss Carolyn had gotten him some thick sliced bacon and he pulled out a pan and threw it in. In moments, it was sizzling. Greta pushed the door open and started what looked to Hades like a systematic search of the premises.

She lay down in the kitchen and watched the bacon in the pan. Hades got some eggs out and found a depression era toaster and some bread. He could bake his own bread, once he really got settled. Maybe plant a garden too. One thing was sure, he wouldn't have to worry about deer and rabbits if Greta stayed around.

He crisped half the bacon and left the other half near raw for Greta. He set them aside on two plates to cool. He siphoned off most of the grease into a can on the sink and then added the eggs.

"Easy over or well done, girl?"

Her tail thumped twice and he put some eggs once they were finished, on her plate and his. The toast, he didn't share. No use in getting her into bad habits. He carried the plates outside and they ate together in the cool morning air under the shade of the mountain ridge. Greta closed her eyes and rolled back on her side. She damned near took up half the porch.

"I have to go into town and collect the news, Greta. I'll leave the door open if you want to nap inside." He felt stupid even as he said it. Why would a wolf want to be inside? She stared at him through golden slitted eyes and then lay her head back down.

Hades saw that Carolyn's car wasn't at the church yet and he wondered how early it was. It seemed that she should be there. He would have to talk to her about his suspicions later.

He glanced in the mirror and saw the big wolf moving off the porch into the splotched sunlight of the hill behind the cabin.

The drive was peaceful and he was glad to see there was a good crowd at the coffee house. He ordered another breakfast with a good dose of guilt and sat down to nurse his coffee. A fair number of people stopped by to chat. None of them knew any more than he did but he planted seeds here and there.

He was ready to give up on the coffee shop and go back to speak to Miss Carolyn when Carson Smith came in. His head darted from side to side looking for someone he knew. He noted the Friar but passed over him as not his first choice. The Friar knew when he'd gotten to the end of the list because he grabbed a cup of coffee and sat down with Hades.

"I can see you debating whether to leave or not. I wish you'd stay for a minute." Carson said with a smile.

"Do you really care what any of these people think about you?"

"No, but I care what you think. You aren't like these yokels; you're more like me."

"Not even." Hades shook his head and made to get up. He forced himself to sit back down. Any information Carson let slip could help. The coffee was churning in his gut.

"No, you might not see it, but it's clear to me. We're both predators. Everyone else is prey. We stride while others cower. Plot and plan while others sleep. I think maybe you and I want the same thing for this town."

"And what would that be?"

"Me out of it and back to New York. I don't know if you heard, but I'm tethered here as punishment for transgressions we don't need to get into. "

"How can I help?"

"I'm not sure you can. I just want you to be aware that everything I do is to get back to New York."

"Does that include hurting those girls?"

"No, of course not." Carson laughed as if it was the most ridiculous thing in the world. He looked around the shop to see who might be watching him.

"It's easier to do what you do in a big city, isn't it? Girls go missing all the time." Hades appeared to be considering the benefits.

"Stop. Well, it looks like this trip has been wasted." He got up and nodded to a few people, then left.

Hades brow furrowed. Something was wrong. Carson Smith seemed nervous. He was concerned with people seeing him. It screamed alibi.

Hades brought his cup to the counter and went to the window to watch Carson get in his silver Lexus.

He headed out of town toward the church. Hades started towards the door, then caught himself. What was he doing? It wasn't his place to drive Carson to ground. The Sheriff could do that. He should sit and have his coffee.

"He's always been a queer one," an old man in a flannel shirt came and stood by him at the window.

"I'm concerned he had something to do with those girls. I'm just not sure it's my place to go beat a confession out of him," Hades admitted. He'd seen the man in the coffee shop, a regular, but had never spoken to him.

"Wouldn't surprise me at all. Always been a creeper. But, you won't be doing yourself no favors buttin' into town business, that's for sure. We take care of our own and we take care of our own, if you know what I mean." The emphasis shifted from comfort to menace.

Hades understood how it worked. Like the platoon: they watched out for their own and they exacted punishment for their own by their own standards. He nodded.

"Guess I'll go back and see if Miss Carolyn is in yet."

"She didn't come in for her coffee this morning. She's usually like clock work. She lives in the big white house at the end of Main Street so she usually drops right in on her way to the church. Can't remember when I've seen her miss a morning."

Hades fired up the Bronco and sped back to the church. Something bad was going on. He could feel it take momentum like a runaway train.

Miss Carolyn's Caddy wasn't in the church lot. Hades let the Bronco idle while he thought of what to do next. Contact the Sheriff? Hades drove back to town but didn't see the big Suburban at the coffee shop.

# Chapter Fourteen

He drove down Main Street and saw a big white house at the end of the street. It wasn't huge but a nice size for a large family. There were four, two-story pillars in front and a nicely manicured lawn. Enormous maples wearing bright red dwarfed the home. A dainty white metal fence proclaimed the property off limits to plain folk.

A decorative rock the size of a Volkswagen sat in the middle of the drive, an ostentatious nod to their source of their money.

Hades saw Miss Carolyn's Caddy in front of the circular drive. It looked like she was ready to come to work. Maybe she was sick. He came up the drive and jumped out. When knocking on the door produced no results, he tried the front door. It didn't yield to his efforts and he debated walking around the back. He weighed how bad it would look, him sneaking around Miss Carolyn's house versus waiting for the Sheriff.

If she was hurt, he would never forgive himself. He took the pristine white gravel path around to the French doors at the back of the house. He wondered who tended the rigidly set out gardens and who deadheaded the buds when they were past their prime. He would have bet money it wasn't Miss Carolyn.

He surveyed the kitchen through the glass doors and the elegant breakfast nook. A buttered muffin with a generous dollop of something red sat on the table, crumbs trailing across the glass table-top.

Miss Carolyn would never allow such laziness. He searched the pockets of his robe for the cell phone she'd pressed on him. He called the pre-programmed number Miss Carolyn had thoughtfully put in, marvelling that 911 technology hadn't made it to the deep valley of the moraine.

"Sheriff's office," Hades recognized the half deaf woman who worked part-time answering the phone at the Sheriff's office.

"Is the Sheriff around?" He almost yelled to accommodate her hearing loss.

"He's over at the Grabel's picking up a raccoon they shot. Going to test it to see if it's got rabies."

"Can you tell him to come right away to Miss Carolyn's house?"

"Miss Carolyn's house? Is something wrong?" Her hearing seemed to have improved at the mention of Miss Carolyn.

"Maybe. She didn't make it to work. Her car is here and I'm looking in the back windows and she left food on the table, half eaten. I'm worried she may have fallen and is hurt but I don't want to break into her home," he relayed the entirety of what he knew because he knew she would require all the details anyway. He may as well get it over with up front. If Carolyn needed help, it would speed things up.

"He'll be right over. Out," Hades was listening to dead air for a moment before he realized she had disconnected. He walked back to the front and then over to the garage at the side of the house. He tested the overhead double door and then followed the garage around to the side and tried the side door.

He was surprised it took the Sheriff so long to arrive. He assumed the operator would've told him to hurry. Someone else was in the front of the car with him.

A small white woman with a cap of silver hair got out of the Suburban. She pulled out a key and hurried to the garage.

"Netty, try the front door," The Sheriff said.

"Well, I'm not allowed to go in the front door," she seemed confused.

"I'll tell Miss Carolyn I made you and I'll apologize personally if I have offended her. Now open the front door," he boomed.

The Sheriff nodded at Hades. "Thanks for the call. I can't remember when Miss Carolyn hasn't made it to the coffee shop in the morning."

Netty opened the door and stepped aside to let the Sheriff and Hades enter first.

"How come you weren't here?" Hades asked the woman.

"She don't like me here if she ain't here. She's always got to be here."

Hades nodded and led them to the back of the house to the kitchen.

Netty gasped.

"What?" said the Sheriff.

"That ain't right. She don't never leave a plate out. Everything's got to be perfect all the time for Miss Carolyn." Netty hurried forward as if to scoop up the offending plate but Hades barred her way.

"It might be evidence," he said gently.

Netty gasped.

"Netty, you go wait outside while the Friar and I search the house."

"I should probably wait outside too," Hades offered after Netty left.

"No, you're sharp. If you weren't a man of the wool, I'd deputize you. You can stay right with me and point out anything I might miss. You can't have too many eyes on something like this."

They went up the spacious stairs after checking all the rooms on the front floor. Hades was amazed at the space and wealth in the house; all for one person. It seemed obscene to him somehow. Like sin made whole and tangible. He liked Miss Carolyn less and less with each step he took.

"All these antiques," Hades shook his head.

"You've got to remember, they were probably the newest in thing when her great great great whatever built this house. They're just antiques because they're old, but they came with the house."

The upstairs consisted of four bedrooms and two full baths. All perfect and all empty. Hades imagined Netty cleaning and Miss Carolyn following behind her criticizing.

"Not here," the Sheriff said finally.

"Let's check the grounds. Maybe she saw something when she was having breakfast and had a heart attack."

"My God, this town will fold without her. There has always been a Bennington in the white house at the end of Main since the town was created. What do you think happened to her?" The Sheriff fumbled for a smoke as they went outside.

"I feel weird about this. You were right to call me, Friar. Like this, I wouldn't be smoking on her property, even the driveway, if I really felt she was here. Something bad has happened."

He and Hades walked the yard including following a small creek in the back.

"Crap, I have to call that brother of hers. He's a yeller."

"Netty, what shoes would she have been wearing? Do you know? Did she have a handbag she always took with her? We need to locate that stuff. I think it's time to call in the FBI. They have manpower and resources we don't. They know how to deal with bodies and missing people; they do it on a regular basis."

The Sheriff wiped the sweat off his forehead. "I think you're right. I'm going to go back to the office and place that call."

"Netty, can you lock up? Sheriff, if you have any crime scene tape, I would put it on the front of the door so no one goes in and screws up any potential evidence."

"Nah, I haven't got any of that stuff."

"Preacher, no one goes in there but me anyway," Netty told them.

"Well, someone else was probably in there this morning," Hades said.

He found her purse in the Caddy and Netty couldn't be sure what shoes she might wear on any given day.

"You might want to get her phone records and see who she called and who might have called her." Hades wasn't an expert in investigating but he'd staged a few crime scenes in his time in the Army. It was a matter of giving the investigator what they thought they would find. Then, they didn't look any further.

He wanted to make sure that didn't happen with Miss Carolyn.

"Sheriff, you might tell Miss Carolyn's brother to light a fire under the FBI, if he knows anyone over there. They might move a lot faster with a push." Random ideas floated through his mind from another time, another place. A time when he had to consider all possibilities and plan for as many contingencies as he could imagine.

Hades thought that was all behind him. That when he turned in his camo and rifles, he could forget that state of mind that came over him. The deadly stillness of the hunter, a fine focus that eliminated all distraction. He felt the calm stillness now and knew he would join the hunt actively instead of trying to orchestrate it from the sidelines.

Did hunting this man conflict with his vows? Obedience, no as long as he didn't ask permission from anyone. Chastity, hardly. Poverty, he wasn't doing it for material gain but to stop the killing. It was good all around.

Hades stopped back at the church and rummaged till he found the address for Barrington in the church files. Driving past he didn't see the Lexus in front. He pulled the Bronco into the drive and killed the engine. He was fairly certain Carson didn't do his own lawn work. In his estimation, no one did. The lawn was huge, but unkempt. Weeds had taken control and it looked like they were moving on to the house. A stack of magazines yellowed with age, littered the stoop.

It fit with what he knew about Carson. If his daddy wouldn't pay for it, he wouldn't keep up the appearances that were so important to his family.

The house had an abandoned feel about it except that he knew Carson lived there. It was as empty as Carson's soul, thought Hades. Too bad he couldn't save him. The thought stopped him into stillness for an instant. Who said he couldn't save Carson? God certainly wasn't putting any constraints on him. It was only his own weakness that stopped him, that and one dead girl and another thrown in a hole. And maybe, just maybe Miss Carolyn. He had to get past the searing anger that thundered in his veins.

If Miss Carolyn was in danger, he needed to help her. If Carson had anything to do with it, and he was sure he did, he might have a captive audience when he was in jail.

Hades smiled, the bad side of his face stiff and not moving. He might be able to save Carson yet. The idea appealed to him. He knocked on the door. "Carson."

There was no answer not that he expected one. He took a quick look around, he couldn't be seen from the street. The large overgrown yard shielded him from unwanted inspection. He ducked around the side of the house and peered into the dirty windows. He didn't see anyone. The inside of the house was a mess too. Who lived like this?

Nobody was home, he concluded. Where else would he take her? He needed a local to help him out. No one was more local than Petri Thomas. Plus, she had the advantage of being home.

He drove over to her house and saw her picking some dead leaves out of her empty flower boxes. She waved at him.

"Petri, how are you?"

"Still sucking air. What's up in town?"

"Miss Carolyn is missing. I think Carson took her. I need to know where he might go. Any ideas?" He sat on her stoop. She sat down next to him with a thump.

"Lord, there's so many access roads for when they used to log and then the mining roads. There's just no way to say." She took her hat off and blew out some air.

"If you had to guess, where would he go?" It reassured him that she didn't question his allegation that Carson had taken Miss Carolyn.

"If I had to say, I'd say a mining road. He hates his father so much."

"Where are they located?"

"Well most of them are on the way out of town towards the north, I'd say. If he was dumping her, he'd use one of those that's easy on easy off."

"Get rid of her right away. I see what you're saying. Damn. I hope he isn't going to hurt her." Hades thought about it. "Thanks." He got up and got back in the Bronco. He headed out of town, moving slowly, scanning the woods for signs of fresh movement.

He stopped when he saw a likely access road, got out and looked for fresh sign of a vehicle passing.

Nothing that he could see. He decided he would hunt better on foot and took off at a jog he could keep up all day if he had to. He remembered when he escaped in the desert. He had run for what seemed like days. He hunted better on foot than in a car.

While he ran, he prayed for God's help in finding Miss Carolyn before she was hurt. Sometimes when he prayed he felt God's presence with him. Today, it wasn't like that. He felt nothing, no help from God and he feared for Miss Carolyn. She was hot like radioactive uranium. Carson couldn't afford to keep her alive long.

He ran on, scanning the ground as he went. He stopped five more times to examine roads off to the side for trace. On the sixth road, the grass was bent deeply and he could see tire tracks running into the deep woods. He turned in and almost immediately found the rolled up rug. Hades unrolled it until he exposed the slightly broken body of Miss Carolyn, her head angled oddly and coated with blood. No chance she was alive. He pulled out his cell phone and tried to call the Sheriff. The ridges blocked the signal.

Damn, he was on his own. Was his responsibility to find and root out evil or notify the Sheriff. He sighed when he came to the decision that he really was in the wrong if he didn't notify the Sheriff. It was already too late for Miss Carolyn. Hades doubted Carson would grab another woman today. He would need to lie low for at least a few days. Hades had time to hunt and dispose of him if things didn't work out the way he wanted them.

Maybe he could do both. If he went back to his Bronco, he could manage both; keep an eye out for the silver Lexus and head in the general direction where he could call the Sheriff. Leaving the body probably wasn't the greatest procedure, but he wasn't a cop. In his experience with bodies, the best thing to do was leave the area as quickly as possible.

# Chapter Fifteen

"Fuck, fuck, fucking wolf! God, I hope the church caught. I should go back and run that dog over." So incensed was Carson at the ruin of his handiwork, he spun the wheel and went back to find the wolf.

When he got to the church, he realized his fears were unfounded. The wolf hadn't screwed up anything. The church was burning with a ferocity even he hadn't expected.

Flames danced up the walls and the sound was glorious, like a sizzle and a high-pitched scream combined. It wasn't the first thing he had burned, not by far, but it was his most satisfying. He remembered burning down an annoying neighbor's garage when they lived outside of New York City. When the pain cans went, it was like the Fourth of July. He could only hope the shed here went up the same.

Could he afford the time to watch it? He looked around. The smoke was thick and black. He had better move on before the volunteer fire department came. What a joke they were.

Too bad he couldn't stay, but he had to get moving. He had to stop by his house to pick up some things before he headed out. Clothes, some things he could pawn for cash. Should he alert dear old dad that the shit was hitting the fan? Would it help or hurt his case? Maybe if daddy didn't know where he was, he might be worried about him. Probably not, but couldn't hurt to give it a shot.

He drove in a big circle keeping his gaze on the inferno. The ridge was dry, he really hoped it went up. Let them all jump in their precious quarry to save themselves.

# Chapter Sixteen

"Hey, you see that black smoke over to the North?" Old Man Johnson limped into the coffee shop and yelled to no one in particular. Everyone left their coffee where it was and streamed to the door.

"Looks like where the church is," remarked an observer.

"I guess we better get the fire truck and head out there," the waitress said.

"That church will go up like a match head. It's all wood," said Johnson.

"Let's get at it." one of the men spoke and they all got in their trucks to go to the firehouse and pick up the truck, sand, shovels and axes with which to fight the fire.

In exactly 12 minutes, the fire truck went out of the garage and calls had been made to surrounding towns for help.

The women in town were making food and brewing coffee for the crews.

By the time most of the town had assembled to fight the fire, the cabin was engulfed and the ridge was starting to smolder.

Martin Sanders, the fire chief, was organizing the men into squads and assigning them areas.

"The church is lost. We'll concentrate on keeping the ridge from burning. Let's get above it but be careful not to get caught by the fire. The air currents will be bringing the fire up to us, so try to fight it from the side. Let's move and beat this thing."

"Men with shovels, dig a fire break on the far side of the church. Maybe we can contain it.

The men moved without complaint, knowing the fire could threaten their homes just as easily as the church. The Bronco roared up into the church parking lot.

Hades parked across the street and ran up, his mouth set in a grim line of anger.

"Do we know what happened?"

"Betting on arson, but we won't know till the state boys get here. Shit, I haven't even called them yet. Put that on the to do list," said Martin

"I'm betting Carson did this."

"If he did, he better pray it doesn't turn into a wildfire. The wind will take this fire up on top and then it's off to the races and no one is going to be able to stop it." Martin took his shovel and headed up the ridge.

Hades was conflicted: should he help or hunt the douche bag who did this?

The Sheriff pulled up and parked behind Hades.

"What the hell?"

"Martin thinks it's arson. I'm thinking it's Carson. He's getting desperate. Did you get my message?"

"Yeh I was just on my way out there. Your directions are spot on. You saw Miss Carolyn's body?"

"Looked like her skull was bashed in."

"Why don't you take me there? Looks like they got enough manpower to handle this."

The Sheriff drove and Hades pointed out where he'd seen the rug and body.

As the Sheriff began to pull into the road, Hades said, "You might want to park on the other side in case there are tire tracks they can match or if he dropped something."

They pulled into a spot across the street and they walked over together.

"The biggest crime we had up to now is a stolen bike or two. Now, we've had two murders and an attempted. You seem pretty set on Carson as our guy."

"He just hits all the lights. I would bet my life on him being our guy. He just feels wrong. He's angry and I think he's snapped."

They looked over the scene and the Sheriff took a few pictures to send to the FBI.

"This is beyond me. I'm bringing in the big guys."

"Probably a good idea. That's what I'd do," lied Hades. Lying was a venial sin. He wished he hadn't done it, especially to the Sheriff.

"I lied. I wouldn't call the FBI. I'd probably try to handle it myself. I'm too used to being out there by myself with no one for backup. The smart thing to do would be to call the FBI." He would have to hit the confessional hard this week.

"Kind of figured you for a lone wolf. I'll make that call."

"Where do you think Carson is?"

"No idea."

"I think if I was him, I'd head out of town. Two bodies and a girl who may or may not remember me, He's got to leave and hope daddy can smooth it over from afar." They walked back to the car.

"I've got to drive back into town to get reception. Best if you came with to stay out of trouble."

"Drop me off here. I'll help with the fire fighters," Hades told him. The air was heated and dark oily smoke swirled the smoke like a small tornado in the valley.

"Thanks. For helping," the Sheriff was wheezing. "I'm going to head over and call from the office. Maybe turn on the air. Can you call me if anything exciting happens?"

"Absolutely. Is there a shovel in this thing I could borrow?" Hades got out and went to the back of the Suburban after the Sheriff pointed him there.

A heavy-duty shovel, brand new was lashed into the back compartment. Hades pried it loose and slammed the door, waving to the Sheriff. He went to the cabin, which was smoking from the roof but hadn't caught yet, to get his things. The truck had soaked the small building and the wood on the porch slipped under his sandals. Hades filled up his duffle with his Bible, running clothes and a few other things, grabbing his boots on the way out. He sat on someone's bumper and put on heavy wool socks and his work boots.

A battered, yellow school bus pulled up as the Sheriff roared off. Its brakes squealed for so long, Hades began to move away from its path. Men tumbled out of the bus holding axes and shovels. They stood in a large group waiting for direction. A small man in blaze orange came out of the bus with a cell phone next to his ear. It had to be hard to hear over the roar of the fire. Hades looked at where the church had been when the smoke moved away in the wind for a second. There was a dark and oily burn mark on the ground and a few upright sticks left. He shook his head.

The man with the cell phone waved the men together. Hades headed over to hear the instructions.

"It's almost atop the ridge, Jed wants us to go into town and start cutting and trenching on the other side to protect the coffee shop. He doesn't think they're going to be able to stop it on their side. He's planning on pulling everyone back down the other side when it jumps the trenches. So, let's get back on the bus and we'll get over there. I'll let the water truck know where to come." He dialed another number and bent to shield the phone from the noise. The men trooped back on the bus and Hades got on too.

Ten minutes later, they got out in the parking lot of the coffee shop. As men got off the bus, they cast worried eyes up the ridge. Hades did the same. He marvelled at the primordial fear that coursed through him. He threw his duffle on the porch of the coffee shop and headed up the ridge with the other men.

The hot wind came over the ridge and pushed at his face, making his eyes tear. It buffeted his robe, pushing it against his legs as he climbed. He spit once, knowing as every other man did, exactly how the fire would jump over the ridge and roar down the other side at them, sweeping through the small town like those videos of volcanic ash rushing down valleys and killing everyone. The smell of the burning pines was so thick, Hades could see it as the smoke clung to his heavy robes. It was like incense, mildly unpleasant but pungent.

He was halfway to the top when he saw the line of men with chainsaws starting to cut down trees and digging trenches. They were within sight of the top of the ridge. Most of them were digging parallel trenches and others had chainsaws and were cutting down the trees at the bottom and moving up behind the trench diggers. Hades wondered as he dug if they had called in those helicopters filled with water hanging loose under their bellies like a pregnant cat.

Somehow, by the men's desperation, he doubted it. The people of Fell knew they were all alone and no one would come to help them except their neighbors.

Hades pushed everything out of his mind but a single prayer to God to spare these people, and he dug. Sweat ran down his face, neck and chest under his robe. The ruined side of his face burned where it touched. Hades gritted his teeth as he thought of the pain that flames would cause him. He flashed back to the acid dripping on his face, trying not to scream and worrying if he did survive that he would be a monster.

He realized he didn't have the cell phone which was back in the Bronco near the cabin. When he saw the man in charge of their group walk past, he motioned him over.

"Can you call the Sheriff and let him know how things are? He might want to evacuate the town," Hades yelled to be heard over the chain saws but the man nodded and got out his cell phone.

They dug trenches and then would move to the next higher elevation and began again. The men with chainsaws were working on the bigger trees now and when they fell, the ground shook like it was an earthquake. The giants lay heavily next to each other on the hill. Hades wondered about the wisdom of this system but then he heard the growling of a big engine and saw a couple of men and a woman driving their tractors over to drag the logs to the other side of the parking lot.

Hades marvelled at their efficiency and teamwork. There must have been other fires in the area before although he hadn't seen any evidence of it.

Hades felt the pounding before he heard it or saw the men streaming over the ridge. They weren't running exactly but allowing themselves to do a controlled jog down the ridge.

The flames arced up behind the ridge and the wind sucked up the unburnt side to meet it. Choking smoke rushed back down the hill and men ran down to the parking lot, coughing. Hades thought he could keep digging but a man going past him touched his shoulder and pointed down the hill.

He saw a tanker truck pulling into the parking lot at the base of the hill. Firemen lept down and began putting hoses together. The men who had been working on the hill drank cold water from plastic cups brought out by the grateful waitress of the coffee shop.

She took one look up the hill and ran to get her keys and move her car.

Hades saw the Sheriff pull up and walked over to his open window.

"Shit," the Sheriff croaked, his voice barely a whisper.

"Yeah, that about covers it," said Hades. He took another drink of the cold clear water, frowning at the dark flakes of ash that floated on the top of the cup.

"Jump in. We've got to let everyone know to evacuate. The ambulance is taking care of the shut ins but I need someone on the loudspeaker."

"I should really stay here and help dig. They need every able-bodied man."

"There's another two tankers on the way. These guys will just be sitting around getting their breath for the next hour. You may as well come with me. We can finish the close in streets and even most of the outlying ones in an hour."

Hades looked around and saw the men relaxing while the tanker lined up to spray on the fire. He got into the Suburban.

"We can hit most of the town with about eight streets," the Sheriff told him as he drove. "You hold the mic and press this button to speak."

"What do you want me to say?"

"Mandatory evacuation. A wildfire is spreading towards the town. I think that ought to do it." The Sheriff slowed down and handed Hades the mic.

Hades repeated the message several times on each street until he wasn't sure of its meaning anymore. They moved farther out from the center of town and he repeated it less often as the houses grew sparse.

"Hey, isn't this Barrington's street?" Hades recognized it from his last visit although he didn't want to say so.

"Sure is, looks like his car in the driveway too." They drove slowly past. The Sheriff turned around in the cul-de-sac.

"Perhaps we should make sure he gets evacuated properly."

"Like in cuffs." The Sheriff pulled behind the silver Lexus, blocking its exit.

They both got out and Hades looked carefully for signs of Carson. This was the worst kind of situation, a cornered desperate man, probably armed and aware they were coming. Crap, they'd been announcing their presence for almost forty minutes all across town. He had to know they were there, was almost certainly watching them and planning an ambush.

"Let me go first," Hades said quietly.

The Sheriff shook his head. "Wouldn't be right. I'm the Sheriff. Hell, I've got the gun unless you're hiding one in that skirt."

Hades smiled. "I'm more used to leading the charge. I don't need a gun; I've got the Lord."

"I don't feel right about that Friar. I should go first."

Hades knew he had him. "I'll go first and you can come behind me with the gun. Maybe we can talk him down. I'd rather avoid any gunfire."

"Know what you mean. I'd be just as happy to take him without any gun play."

Hades moved towards the side of the house. He wanted to move the killing field, to upset his plan if he had one. He moved quickly, silently all of his senses alert.

The Sheriff stayed a decent distance behind him, which he appreciated although he suspected it was more from caution than intelligent strategy.

He glanced into the windows as he moved quickly past them. A glance gave a soldier a snapshot in his mind. Hades was trained in such techniques from his time in the Army.

He tried the knob and found it locked. He thought for a moment. Should he kick it in and then dive for cover? Should he go to the back and hope that door was unlocked? A third choice was to break into a window.

"Sheriff, here's a rock," he said quietly as he handed the Sheriff a large rock. "While you do that, I'm going to kick in the door and dive in."

The Sheriff nodded and pointed to a window halfway up the side of the house. Good, thought Hades, he got the strategy. The distraction might save Hades' life.

He waited till the Sheriff was in position and they moved at the same time. The door caved in easily and threw Hades forward unexpectedly. The sound of the rock breaking the window was startling.

Hades was on his feet moving through the house before the sound died away.

"That's far enough, Friar." Carson was sitting in a wooden chair in the filthy living room, his back in a corner.

By staying calm, he had foiled their plan. Hades smiled. It told him something about his adversary.

The Sheriff came in behind Hades, gun drawn.

"Drop it, Carson," he sounded a million years old with that breathless asthmatic wheeze.

Carson shot him in the shoulder. The explosion of the gun deafened Hades for a moment and he moved to catch the man before he hit the ground. He turned him slightly and checked for an exit wound. There was a wound going out. It was a good thing Carson was using a twenty-two caliber. The Sheriff had an excellent chance of survival. He pulled a table runner off the side table and folded it several times and pressed it to the wound.

"He needs a doctor."

"He's not going to get one. You guys should have left this alone. I was packing to leave. Now, what am I going to do with you?" Carson's voice rose alarmingly.

"Calm down," Hades said, hoping to bring the man down off the adrenaline high of shooting the Sheriff.

"You don't tell me what to do." Carson was waving the gun wildly. ' Hades could only focus on the Sheriff.

"Get him up." Carson ordered.

"He can't be moved," Hades told him.

"Of course he can. Get him up or I'll put him out of my misery."

"Come on, Sheriff. Let's get you up." Hades took his weight and helped him to stand. The Sheriff's face was an ugly gray that worried Hades. He wound a strip of the fabric around the Sheriff's shoulder and tied it to put pressure on the wound.

"Let's take your Suburban. My car is a little too noticeable right now."

Hades helped the Sheriff out to the Suburban. Carson was too far away for Hades to make a play for him. Smart man. Hades wanted nothing more than to rip the man's head off.

"Put him in the front. In fact, you both get in the front."

"I'm not sure he can drive."

"Give me a break. I'm not an idiot. He can drive. If you want to get him to a doctor, do what I say and it will get him there faster."

"You're just going to kill us anyway." He got the Sheriff in the car and then moved around to the shotgun seat and got in. He considered running but he couldn't abandon the Sheriff. "Where are we going," he said wearily.

"Just back out and drive towards the church." Hades turned to look back at Carson, alarmed at how his face was flushed and his eyes looked feverish. The guy was majorly whacked out and was capable of anything, Hades judged.

"Just do it," he told the Sheriff. The Sheriff grunted with pain as he moved the lever to move the Suburban backwards.

The Sheriff drove slowly through the town. It seemed that the town had swelled by hundreds. School buses lined Main Street. The heavy smell of pine suffused the air, tinged with smoke.

It broke Hades' heart to see the town so threatened, his town. He tried to will the Sheriff to crash slowly into a building or have another "safe" accident, but the Sheriff was concentrating so hard on the act of driving that he didn't pick up any of the subtle signals Hades was trying to send.

He debated pulling the wheel and making it happen but decided against it.

They were passing the cabin when Carson said, "Slow down!" Hades turned in his seat and watched Carson's greedy face drink in the wreck of God's church.

"You can't stop God, Carson."

"No, but I stopped you, didn't I?"

"Stopped me from what exactly?"

"Pull in. I want to see the pretty flames." He gestured for the Sheriff to pull in. The gun didn't waver from the back of his seat.

They pulled to a stop on an angle to where the church had been, flanked by trees on two sides. Carson scooted so he was behind the Sheriff and looking out the window nearest the church. The flames had eaten most of the trees on the hill and the cabin was just a dark smudge on the gravel.

Everyone was on the other side of the ridge, battling the fire and they had the scene to themselves for the moment.

"Why did you kill Miss Carolyn?"

"She disagreed with me. I think she was starting to like you, preacher, stink and all. Although now, I must say, you smell wonderful: all woodsy and pine scented. You should appreciate what I'm doing for you." He held the gun steady and watched the flames lick up the hill.

"And the girl, the first one?"

"She was trailer trash," he shrugged. A tall tree sparked as the sap ignited and smoke rose from it like an old time steam engine.

"And the second girl, the one in the hole behind the cabin?" Keep him talking was the first rule of hostage negotiation.

"Do you know how long it took me to dig that fucking hole? I was sure they would blame you. They probably would have if you hadn't found her."

"She's going to be ok," Hades sent up a prayer for the girl and the Sheriff both getting through their encounters with Carson.

"Yeah, well who cares?"

"God cares and he cares about you too," dangerous ground, thought Hades but if he meant to save the idiot's soul, no time like the present.

Another truck pulled in facing them, drivers' door to drivers' door.

"Hey, Sheriff, you ok?" The man's name didn't come to mind immediately. He nodded to Hades and Carson.

Before the Sheriff could comment either way, Carson shot the man through the open window. Blood flew from him against the windshield on the inside. He slumped over. His truck was in Park luckily or he would have hit their vehicle.

"Why'd you have to do that?" The Sheriff rasped. He slid a look at Hades.

"Friar, get out and put him in the back. We can't leave him. Let's get going before someone else stops by that I have to shoot. Because I will shoot them," he promised them.

Hades got out, delaying as long as he could. He walked behind the truck and turned off the engine. He hauled the guy out after making sure the man was dead. Slung him over his shoulder and carried him to the back of the Suburban. He balanced him on one shoulder and opened the door. He made a quick survey of the things in the back of the truck but didn't find anything he could conceal and use later as a weapon. Damn.

He got back in the shotgun seat and sighed.

The Sheriff put it in gear and pulled slowly out. He moaned as he turned the big wheel and got back onto the main road.

"Where are we going?" asked the Sheriff.

"I don't know. Just down the road a piece. We'll find an access road. We have to get rid of the body." Carson was almost hanging out the window like a dog. He scanned the road for a likely spot.

"Pull in here. This looks good."

The Sheriff drove right past it.

"Hey!"

"Sorry, I must have spaced out. What did you want?" The Sheriff was pretending to be worse than he was, Hades hoped. It wasn't a bad strategy but it would only work once.

"Dammit. I'll shoot you right here. Pull off at the next access road."

"OK. Sorry." Hades thought maybe the next access road wouldn't be as beneficial. It was another good delaying tactic and Hades' respect for the Sheriff increased.

The road didn't go far before it became too high for the Suburban to pass without going into four-wheel drive.

"OK, this is good." The Suburban sank back when the Sheriff turned off the car.

Carson sat for a moment and surveyed the area.

"This is good," he began when a blur of gray shot through the back window. Hades heard a grunt as the mass of fur and growl hit Carson. The big wolf hung half in and half out of the window, its hind feet were scrambling for purchase when the boom of the gun echoed painfully in Hades' ears.

Then, the wolf was gone. Carson was screaming and blood was everywhere. Hades could only hope it was Carson's. Hades tried to grab for the gun but Carson fired at him from the back seat. The shot hit the headboard above their heads.

Then, there was silence.

"Where the fuck is that beast?" Carson yelled, his eyes darting from side to side.

"I think she's gone," Hades told him.

"I hope I killed her, stupid wolf." Carson jumped out and retrained the gun on the Sheriff and Hades. "Get the shovel and let's get digging."

Hades went to the back and got the body out and laid it on the ground. He got the shovel, looking around for a soft spot.

# Chapter Seventeen

She trotted from the smoke and fire, instinctively fearing it. The motion was easier than walking and she could maintain this ground eating pace for days. The Strong Man wasn't in the cabin or the other building. She stood at the edge of the clearing watching for him, just in case. She belonged to him; they belonged together. If the Strong Man wasn't aware of it yet, she would instruct him. She paused and licked a paw.

A car came into the clearing and she wondered if Strong Man might be inside. Her ears stood up and her tail made a tentative wag.

Then, all thoughts of Strong Man left her, the malodorous scent of Bad Thing filled her sensitive nostrils. Her vision was acute but she waited a moment for confirmation from tiny particles floating to her on the air. Her ability to read a scene from the nuances of scent was unparalleled.

The same sweet alcohol odor was in the air when Long time Man died. The slab of meat that she'd wanted so much had his remnants on it. She'd wanted the fresh meat but recoiled from the tainted scent. She hated him from that moment and associated him with hate, anger and the death of Longtime Man.

Had he eaten the tainted meat? She had smelled his lips and hadn't sensed the taint, but he could have eaten it earlier. If it was in his stomach, she might not recognize it. She decided the man who smelled like this combination of sickly sweetness and fear had killed Long Time Man.

She would hunt him in the manner of her kind. She would track him forever, if that's what it took. She was a patient and talented hunter and was confident she would run across his trace sooner or later. The scent was imprinted in her brain pan permanently. There was no escape from her.

Now the scent of Strong Man reached her. If he was with Bad Thing then she had to help him. Bad Thing had killed Long Time Man and she wasn't going to lose another pack member to this Evil. Another man was in the front seat bleeding. The coppery rich scent on him and it almost masked his own scent but she searched her memory: it was someone the Long Time Man had over once in a while. He'd drunk beer with them on occasion and made Long Time Man laugh.

She trotted towards the vehicle, circling downwind so Bad Thing wouldn't smell her. Although men were notoriously inept hunters, she wouldn't take any chances with Bad Thing.

To get to him in the back seat, she would have to enter through the window. A tight fit for her huge body but she could do it and perhaps drag him back out with her. The problem was that she would have to cross forty feet of open gravel to get in striking position.

She crouched to begin the sprint when another vehicle came into the clearing and almost butted up against the one with Bad Thing and Strong Man in it. She lay down to wait in the camouflage of the pines. Strong man wasn't in danger right now, but she was ready to move in the space of a heart beat.

She heard the crackle before the heat. The explosion ripped through the air in front of her and she was up and running. Her delicate ears hurt and she ran for ten yards before she made herself stop. Then she turned back and watched from where she was. Strong Man was in trouble.

She leaned her nose up into the air drafts and found blood, urine and death. Strong Man got out of the car. He went to the other car and pulled the dead meat out and put it in their car. For later? Hard to say. She licked her lips hoping Strong Man would feed her eggs and bacon again. Sharing food was how the pack worked. If Bad Thing was there, she would refuse to eat and then challenge him later.

She would feel his blood flow over her lips, pack or no.

The car with the living men in it, made a big circle in the gravel and drove onto the highway heading away from town. She debated following, looking back at the smoking hills and then at the retreating car.

She went into her soft lope and followed the car down the road.

### 

His head swiveled constantly and Hades laughed when he realized Carson was looking for the wolf. He was right to look. Greta wasn't likely to slink away, unavenged.

Hades went to the back and got the body out and laid it on the ground gently. He went back and got the shovel, looking around for a soft spot.

By the time he was ready, the Sheriff had climbed painfully out and was leaning against the side of the vehicle. Carson had circled the car once and was looking up into the dense trees that covered the access area.

"Dear God in heaven," Hades began.

"Knock that crap off. Just bury him."

Hades shook his head gently. "No can do. My boss is pretty firm about this stuff. He ignored Carson as the man waved the gun and yelled. He continued the service until he was confident he had done his best for the man before him. Even in the direst times, how people treated their dead bespoke volumes of their humanity.

Hades measured the distance between him and Carson. Too far for a big shovel swing. The man hadn't lost it yet. He was bleeding from puncture wounds in his jaw and neck where Greta had tried to separate his head from his shoulders. Hades smiled when he considered the amount of bacteria in a wolf's mouth.

He took his time digging, making the hole perfect. He squared off the corners expertly.

"Oh, for God's sake, just dig the hole. Delaying won't get the Sheriff any closer to medical care."

"You know, Carson," the Sheriff rasped, "When you lie, your voice gets higher." The Sheriff barked a laugh, dissolving into a wet coughing fit.

"Shut up, you imbecile. You never would have figured out it was me if it wasn't for the stupid Friar."

"Maybe not, but the feds would. One body, they might ignore but they seemed pretty interested in two and an attempted third," the Sheriff took a step forward and Hades said a silent blessing. He knew that he was trying to give Hades the opportunity he needed to make a last desperate play before Carson killed them both.

"That's good enough. Put the nosey bastard in first." Carson motioned to the dead man. There was just a hint of piney smoke in the air but a haze was across the sky and the three of them stood ringed around the shallow, leaf filled grave in a semi gloom although it was just before noon.

Carson stood before them with his back to the woods. Blood from his puncture wounds had dried on his face and Hades thought he looked like a painting that had begun to melt in the heat.

The Sheriff was to Hades right and they formed a loose triangle. Hades took the corpse's feet and dragged them into the hole. It slid on the slick leaves and he walked around to pick up the shoulders.

Hades heard a low quiet cough and smiled inside. Greta. She would be the tiebreaker in this. Carson feared her and with good reason. For whatever reason the wolf decided she wanted to kill him, Hades was grateful.

Greta might provide just the distraction he needed to go hand to hand with Carson. The man wouldn't have a chance, he vowed.

"Carson, can we get the Sheriff to an ambulance now? We've done everything you asked."

"He ain't gonna let us get to no doctor, son. He's a liar, just like his dad before him." The Sheriff rasped out.

"My dad is not a liar," the gun wavered between the Sheriff and Hades. Who did Carson hate more and would Greta cooperate and take the cue?

The Sheriff laughed until he wheezed and dissolved into a coughing fit. "He was the biggest fucking liar this town has ever seen."

Hades dropped the corpse's shoulders on the ground again, stumbling a little as he did. "What do you mean, Sheriff?" Carson said.

In dropping the man's shoulders, Hades took a stumbling side step towards Carson. Carson was fixated on the Sheriff clearing his throat.

"Well, your sainted father stole the land rights for his sainted mine."

"That's bullshit. The Smiths owned that land since God created it."

"There you go bringing God into it again," said Hades as he turned towards Carson. The turn brought him six inches closer.

"Who owned it before your father though, that's the real question? There were real live people on that land, son. He told them they may have owned the land but he owned the mineral rights. Had some fancy lawyer from New York to back him up." The Sheriff took another step towards Carson too. Hades knew what he was up to. He wanted to be the distraction, the sacrifice so Hades could jump Carson.

Hades knew it might be their only option but he hated it. He was almost ready to leap when an impossibly low rumble began. Carson spun away from them, looking for the wolf. He pivoted back to them as Hades bent his knees.

"It's that fucking wolf," he screamed backing towards the car and closer to Hades.

"You, throw that body in the hole now and then move away," Carson yelled at Hades. The asshole still hadn't lost his cool yet, Hades swore.

He bent down and slid the corpse into the hole. It slid on the wet leaves and the scent of each layer of undisturbed summer floated up to him. He hadn't saved any souls. He hadn't even got a chance to start his mission for God before it had ended here under this leafy bower. He could have wept.

"And you, I don't care if my dad was a crook. He was smarter than everyone else. They were the dumb shits, you old wheezing fucker. Move!" The last was directed at Hades. He moved to the far side of the clearing.

Carson got into the car and started the engine. Hades had a moment when he thought he and the Sheriff might survive but it was short lived when Carson pointed the gun at him out the window of the car. The Sheriff slumped heavily on his butt into the leaves, all the fight worn out of him.

An eerie howl reverberated across the hills. It was loud and Hades felt like it moved his inner ear drum at a certain reverberation that shivered fear down his spine. It wasn't a sad lonely wolf call, it was an angry call to battle.

When Carson looked out the left window, Hades took three quick steps and dove through from the right, both hands clutching for the gun. He felt rather than saw the wolf join the fight. The impact jarred the huge Suburban and made the one hand that Hades had gotten on the gun loose.

The snarling was terrifying in the enclosed front of the car and Hades pulled his arm back more than once rather than rise Greta's bite.

The gun fired, deafening Hades and he heard Greta yelp and sag. Carson started to laugh, a wet sickening sound. Hades put one hand behind Carson's head and another on his chin and snapped his neck in one fluid motion.

He dragged the body out and threw it in the back seat. He picked up the body in the hole dind laid it on top of him. He saw the blood streaking Greta's fun and moved the deep fur, He hoped it was only a flesh wound. A Friar could use a wolf. The idea made him smile when he thought of how the Friary would react to Hades having a wolf as a companion.

He bent down near the Sheriff.

"Can I give you a hand?"

"Not like the one you gave Carson, I hope."

"Not hardly. First stop, hospital for you and then the vet and after that the morgue." He guided the Sheriff to the back seat and helped him in. The Sheriff's side was wet with blood.

"I hope there is one. The fire may have run through town and taken it all."

"When were the feds supposed to come in?" Hades put the car in gear and floored it, spitting chunks of dirt as he drove off the access road.

"Shit, I don't know. They don't tell us dumb local yokels nothing." He spit out the back window.

Greta moaned and Hades dropped one hand to rub her coarse neck. "We'll get you to a vet soon, sweetie," he crooned. They flew past where the church had stood. Hades felt his teeth clench as the sight of the smoldering ashes of the church and the cabin. The hill was burnt earth with smoking piles of branches strewn about like pieces of a children's game.

Hades imagined it would be decades to reforest this area.

He said a fervent prayer that no lives had been lost other than the one in his truck. It was such a waste. He had so much more work to do here. There were the Fellows sisters. He hadn't gotten around to having the discussion about their immortal souls yet. One couldn't rush into these sensitive topics.

Then, there was the Sheriff. He took the measure of the man and he was solid as granite. Hades admitted he'd misjudged him. Wouldn't happen again. An important soul to save, assuming the old man lived.

They went past the diner and Hades was happy to see that it looked like it had mostly survived the inferno. Men were packing up their gear and getting onto their buses.

He drove down Main Street and saw people unpacking their cars and kids. It was going to be alright.

"Turn here, it's a shortcut to the hospital."

"You going to make it, old timer?"

"Me? Nothing can kill me if my wife's cooking hasn't. Maybe you could give her a call and let her know I'm here. We live in the blue house next to the library on Main"

"Will do."

He pulled into the emergency lane and a man and a woman in scrubs ran out with a gurney to take the Sheriff to the Emergency Room. They lifted him out gently but quickly.

"Anyone else?" The male said. He was Latino with a pencil thin mustache and arms the size of tree trunks in a powder blue set of scrubs. By comparison, the woman was petite with pulled back gray hair and thin arms with a purple set of scrubs. They both looked fit

"I've got two dead bodies here."

"They go to the morgue, follow the signs around the corner," he directed with his arm.

"How about you? You don't look so hot. Want to get checked over?" The gray haired woman asked.

"No thanks. How about some antiseptic and gauze for my friend here. She saved my life."

They looked over the front seat and jumped back. "Shit. Is that a wolf?" The man asked.

"Nah, she a huskie, she's just big-boned." They backed warily away without taking their eyes from the vehicle. Moments later, the older woman came out with a bottle of antiseptic, some gauze and a shot. She gave the small bundle to Hades.

"Here, hold this." She took the bottle and poured some onto the gauze. "Hold her head down, will you?" Without waiting, she began to daub the antiseptic on the side of the wounded animal.

Greta half moaned, half growled and the woman crooned nonsense words to her. Greta talked back and they had a very interesting conversation while he stroked her neck.

"Superficial wound from a bullet, I'd say. More a burn than anything. Here are some antibiotic pills you can give to her in liver sausage. She should be fine in a few days. I'll take that needle now. I don't think it will help to wrap it; she'll take it off and lick it anyway." She pulled up a fold of loose skin and stuck the needle in, emptying it in one fluid motion. Greta didn't even seem to notice. "She's beautiful. Wasn't she James Cannon's?"

"Yes, she hunted down Carson and saved the Sheriff and me from being shot. Thanks for helping."

"I'd say stick around, the police will want to talk to you, but you brought in our Sheriff. I imagine he'll talk to you when he is good and ready." The woman kept up a steady chatter as she checked over Greta for other injuries.

"I'll let the Sheriff's wife know he's here, after I drop off these, ah, men." He meant to say bodies but it seemed disrespectful to the man whose name he still didn't know.

He drove around and brought the bodies to the morgue.

The morgue attendant supplied the man's name without Hades even asking.

"Aw, Banner. This is bad."

"I didn't know him. Is it Mr. Banner or is that his first name?"

"It's Mark Banner. He's a nice guy or was. We'll have to find a new dentist that's for sure."

"Does he have a wife I should notify?" Hades helped him move the body to a gurney. They wheeled it through double steel doors that pushed easily open. The morgue had white walls and white linoleum floors. It would have driven Hades nuts to work there.

"No. I expect when his dental assistant finds out he's dead, she'll notify the family. Either that or the Sheriff."

"Sheriff's in the emergency room right now with a bullet in his shoulder from Carson." They walked back out for the other body.

"Now this guy," he said as they lifted Carson Smith onto the next gurney, "I'm not surprised to see. I've been expecting him. He's such an asshat, pardon my French Padre. He's one of those creepy kids who grew up to be a creepy man, in my humble opinion." Hades helped him wheel the remains of Carson into the morgue. They lined up the gurney next to the dentist and stood looking at them.

"I'd hoped to save his soul but I don't think I did him a damned bit of good."

"Padre, you did your best, it wasn't in the cards."

Hades wondered if that were true. He reflected as he drove. What else could he have done to save the dentist from death or Carson from hell?

# Chapter Eighteen

The Sheriff stayed in the hospital for a week and got out just in time for Miss Carolyn's funeral.

"I enjoyed the hospital cooking, that's for sure," he told Hades as they sat on the porch of the rebuilt cabin. His asthma had complicated what would have otherwise been an easy recovery. A smoky smell permeated the air, mixing with the charred pines all around them. The Sheriff pulled on his inhaler.

Carson's body was sent for by his father, no one knew where that funeral was held, if there was one. Banner was the only other casualty and the town mourned their dentist and friend.

Hades looked out at the blackened landscape. There was a stark beauty to it, he decided. He'd been visiting people since the fire and discussing the direction they wanted the town to go from "his" seat at the coffee shop in the evenings. In the mornings, he and a small crew worked on rebuilding the cabin and the church. He would be the spearhead for his God and point them in the right direction.

The funeral for Miss Carolyn drew people from the surrounding communities and Hades presided. They held it in her spacious backyard and garden which she had donated to the town for a museum.

Hades was amazed how many people's lives she had touched, judging by the huge crowd in attendance. His speaking was heartfelt with a touch of humor. He was just one of the long line of speakers celebrating her life.

She left her fortune to the church, administered by a board of trustees which included the "Holy Man in Residence" and Miss Carolyn's brother from New York. Her brother had the majority say in what happened, whenever he chose to use it. They were to meet this week formally but her brother had already made his presence felt.

"We're going to rebuild the church pretty much just how she built it the first time except a bigger choir area and a room for brides to change. There's plenty of money to update your dump of a cabin," he told Hades.

"No, I like it. It is perfect for me just the way we rebuilt it."

"I like you, Hades. Carolyn did too. She told me you were on the odd side but a straight shooter. I think you're just what Fell needs right now. That doesn't mean go hog wild or anything. You could do with a new robe though."

Greta appeared around the side of the cabin and dropped a half-burnt snake at Hades' feet. The wolf looked at him expectantly.

Carolyn's brother recoiled in horror.

"Thanks, girl." Greta took the snake back and began crunching it in her huge mouth.

"Is that a fucking wolf?"

"No, she's just big-boned." Hades smiled.

# About the Author

Dixie Jo Jarchow writes sweet romance and adventure as well as creepy short stories in Black Wolf, WI with her husband of 37 years and her two Boston terriers.

Read more at dixiejojarchow.com.